copyright 2015

www.handoutzine.com

cover photo by
jec

back artwork by
bamn

This book is a work of fiction. All names, characters and incidents portrayed are fictitious. No identification with actual persons (living or deceased), places, buildings, and products is intended or should be inferred.

2

The Day They Razed Our Town

a short story collection

by

Joel

Rochester,
Marietta,
Brooklyn,
NY.

4

contents

The Day They Razed Our Town (6)

Smiling, USA (15)

Ona MOVE (44)

Sophia Sara Bednarczyk (58)

It Was Me (64)

Jesus' Teeth (68)

Taking Short or, I Love You, Chelsea Manning (71)

Bedford & First (106)

Eveline (112)

City Property (117)

Thwack (123)

Jesus used to watch me (127)

At the Beach (129)

Christmas Needs To Come Early This Year (135)

House On Fire (139)

The Day They Razed Our Town

Mom used to run to the front windows to see where the fire trucks or ambulances were heading from the Fire Department just a couple hundred yards from our house. She watched as though if she saw the siren lights ascending Oak Hill she could begin to get some sort of coherent idea of what was on fire or who was hurt somewhere. Oh, they didn't turn on Oak Hill but kept going down Otisco Valley Road, she'd say aloud even to an empty room, seeing the flashing lights become a small spot of light and then vanishing. It might be the Schmidts, she'd say, it might be the Morgans. His heart; her back; their wood house in the lovely cluster of trees by the lake; the road up above the house. What a lawn to mow, up and down and up and down that steep hill; with a push-mower extrememly difficult; with a rider impossible. Maybe GK could do it. $10 a week. $12 if it takes over an hour.

    The only dead body I had ever seen had been carried in a casket – and then it was closed. Dozens of injured bodies were being jostled and transported in the direction of the Community Center (CC). I wondered how so many people could have been hurt or killed without the whole town just being blown up. The bodies were not covered in blood like I expected; only the parts of them which had been struck by bullets. We had heard shots minutes ago and presumed that they were coming from the north, near the cemetery, from where they most often originated.

    Mom and Dad had run outside and were hurriedly talking to anyone who would stop. When Tom King appeared carrying his grandson Mickey, who had been shot in the stomach, Dad picked up

Mickey's lower half and ran down Valley Road with Tom towards the CC, which Tom, a volunteer firefighter, said was serving as town infirmary.

I thought to tell my brother, GK, as we looked out the window, that even though we had lived in Lantern Hill since I was four I did not recognize most of the people running past the house. I did not even know there could *be* so many people who lived in our town. I assumed that they all knew each other, and that we were not a part of the town's larger social world because Dad was the preacher, and there's lots of things people don't do and say around preachers. GK would have poo-poo'd the whole thing, saying something like, 'Whatever, we've been here a decade, Jonah. We know lots of people.'

'I guess anyone who was going anywhere by car is gone,' GK said.

'Yeah, I know.' I rubbed the window with my sleeve to clear what GK called our 'Condensate.' 'I haven't seen one in-'

'Oh my gosh, there's Beth Williams.' She was being carried by her dad, who looked exhausted and terrified. She was our first close friend – her from Sunday school – we had seen wounded.

'Boys, boys,' Mom cried in a strained hush, running back inside. She marched high-steps in the doorway, clenching and unclenching her hands. 'We've got to get you out of here, boys. Boys.'

'What's going on?' I asked.

'They've bulldozed the Mitchell's and all of Cemetery Road. And Jay's Pizza with Jay and Deborah still-' She paused. 'And the bulldozers rolled right over the cemetery-.'

We all lost our breath as Mom began to cry, marching in place. I tried to imagine how many bulldozers could even fit in the cemetery. Maybe three on the one side of Valley Road and two on the other?

Dad entered the house with blood on his shirt and pants and sleeveless arms, his dress shirt still tucked in. We all looked up at the sound of helicopters. Dad placed his hands on Mom's shoulders, saying, 'Frank's picked up some transmissions on the Fire Department scanner. They've bulldozed past the Allen's house. And the helicopters are-' He was silenced by the shuddering sound of the helicopters. Mom shuddered.

The Allen's house was just a half-mile from ours; what Dad called three-quarters of a mile if he wanted to feel good about getting lots of exercise without really getting it.

'Let's go, dear, let's go. Boys, boys.'

'We can't,' Dad said, striking the dinner table with his fist. 'They've blocked Lantern Road at Kinyon and Valley Road at Oak Hill. And they're coming this way from the Allen's.'

'What do we do, dear? What do we do? Boys, boys. Should we go out on the lake? What should we do? We don't even have a boat. Or life-vests. They're probably on the lake, too, dear? Boys, boys.'

'Everyone is going to the Community Center or the Fire Department. If they bulldoze every house in town that's all that's left.'

'What if they bulldoze the Center and the Firehouse, Dad?' I asked. Never had there been so many silences.

At its most congested – the Independence Day parade or Halloween's door-to-door bonanza – Valley Road was hardly trafficked by pedestrians. This was automobile territory. It was exciting to see so many people running and crying and bleeding. So many boobs bouncing, inappropriately and hurriedly harnessed. So many voices shouting orders or questions. So many people who did not know what to do.

Michael Edwards, my friend from Sunday school, who lived well beyond the cemetery, almost to Route 20, ran past us across our front lawn. He held his small digital camera and was recording everyone running to the Center down Valley Road. Maybe he had come the back way, I thought, along the small creek behind the Post Office.

GK shoved me and told me to hurry up, running past me. I chased after him, afraid to look above my head because I thought I might fall and bleed like all of the carried people were bleeding; afraid to look ahead of myself because I wanted to see the helicopters above and try to dodge the bullets, if they shot any.

'Apache Longbow 'copters,' said Kevin Anderson, my next door neighbor and best friend, running beside me out of nowhere. He was, as almost always, good natured, though still frightened. I could tell by how he ran his hand over his buzzed scalp as though wanting to push away the missing locks from his forehead. 'The best 'copters around.'

'How can you tell, Kev?'

'They got the M230 chain gun. See?' He pointed. I nodded, not seeing.

'Why does everyone look so surprised?' Kevin said, turning around to look at everyone. 'My dad saw this coming when they turned off the water yesterday. That's the only reason there's any water at all at the Center.'

The Anderson's backyard was separated from the CC by the large rectangular chain-link fence which ran the entire perimeter of the Center and had always felt more comforting than limiting at the playground. The fence served as an out-of-bounds marker when we played baseball and basketball on the pavement intended for any activity we cared for. 'Dad started filling buckets at the house as soon as the announcement came over the scanner, and then he cut down the fence and started filling buckets at the Center.'

We all screamed, even Kevin, when the guns on the helicopters began firing. Sandra Evans was hit in the head. Instead of falling, it appeared that she continued to run – only her body became horizontal; as though she had run into the ground, which stopped her. People who I had never heard curse before – even 'Oh my God' – began hysterically using all sorts of words.

'Kevin, come on!' Mom called, seeing that he was gawking at the helicopters while she, GK and I raced ahead. 'Where are your parents, Kevin?'

'Aw, they're at the Center already with my sister,' he said, catching up.

It was sometimes difficult for the men (and some women) to carry the injured people for long stretches, and lots of times the carriers fell or dropped the people they carried. The carriers always bounded right back up like a kid would; unless they broke an ankle or something, as Ron Clark had. I hoped that the people being carried were already too far out of things to feel the pain of being dropped.

Turning the corner from Valley Road to Lantern Road the four of us gasped, as had those in front of us and as did those behind us. Once past the Martin's house on the corner we expected to see the highest building in town, which was three stories high and a quarter mile up the steadily but slightly inclining road. Instead we saw – or did not see – that the third floor was missing. The roof was gone entirely and the walls of the second floor were jagged and uneven. It looked like an enormous monster had palmed the building with its huge hand and torn the top off like one might a muffin.

'Those are Mi-28 Havocs,' Kevin said. He did not need to point.

Four helicopters hovered around the apartment building, shooting into it with deafening consistency.

'Those are missiles. Those are missiles all right.' Kevin was the playground expert on military equipment. His dad subscribed to *Guns & Ammo* and *Current History*.

Beyond the apartment building on Lantern Road we saw the roadblock another quarter mile up, where Kinyon Road began, breaking off from Lantern, which turns the corner towards R20. Two camouflaged jeeps and a tank sat behind two sawhorses that stretched across the width of the road. Three soldiers with guns stood in front of the roadblock staring down at us, sunglasses refracting sunlight. Two soldiers appeared from the top of the tank and lit cigarettes.

Kimberly Brown ran past, moving with great swiftness for an elderly woman. 'Like we're not even here. Like I'm not even.' She talked to herself as though she were being interviewed by a very interested reporter. 'Like we're not even here. Like I'm not even a person that weighs anything or has cookies in the oven or wash in the washer-'

'Oh! My banana bread!' Mom cried, turning around to head home. There was not time for GK and I to simultaneously say something sarcastic and laugh before she realized what she was doing and turned around again. She shrugged. 'Well, I've burned it before. Your father will just have to use extra butter.'

We all lost our breath and ran into the gates of the Community Center.

A partial transcript of that evening's 6:00pm local news coverage from Channel 05, WXYZ.

Anchor Thomas Peebles: Coming up, Sports, with Fred Gastoff. We'll see if our Eagles had what it took to defeat the Meadow Voles. But first, according to government officials, in Lantern Hill today government forces, including local police and National Guardsmen, were brought in to find and arrest an alleged terrorist cell in the community. We now go live to Investigative Reporter Dee Dee Perino who is standing outside the safe-house protected by the security forces. Dee Dee.

Investigative Reporter Dee Dee Perino: Tom, I'm standing outside the Lantern Hill Community Center where frightened but safe townspeople have been gathered in preparation for the strike on what officials say is a full blown terrorist cell right here in Lantern Hill. I'm standing here with General John Winthrop, commander of the forces protecting the town and searching for the terrorists. General, what is the purpose of this safe-house and what are you hoping to accomplish by today's actions?

General Winthrop: Firstly we are looking to guarantee the safety and protection of the people of Lantern Valley by searching for and finding the terrorist threat here in town which puts at risk the safety of not only the people of Lantern Hill but of the county at large and perhaps beyond. We are seeking to protect the people of Lantern Valley from the terrorists in town and those who seek to harm it. This was all done using standard counter-terrorism techniques.

Perino: You and your soldiers demolished the town in your search for the terrorist cell's safe-house, is that correct, General?

General Winthrop: That is correct, Maam.

Perino: General, could you expound on that? Explain to people what counter-terrorism is.

General Winthrop: The terrorists in Lantern Hill, more ideologically terrorist than **active/physical** terrorists, were not accustomed to war, were slain by the sword of the Lord. In the morning the terrorists hid in the swamps and we could not find them, so we burnt and spoiled their houses and crops in great abundance. But they kept themselves in obscurity.

Perino: And by afternoon, General?

General Winthrop: By afternoon we maneuvered to the same suspected safe-houses, burnt what was still standing, cut the remainder of useful crops, and destroyed some of their dogs instead of men, since they had left their dogs behind.

Perino: General, are you saying-

General Winthrop: And so in the end that God's name might have the glory, and his people see his power, and magnify his honor for his great goodness.
Perino: General, I'd like to thank you for your time.

Tom, back to you in the studio.

Smiling, USA

I never enjoyed feeding the children. When they talked it didn't make any sense so they never got to tell me if they were hungry. Some of the children could eat so fast I'd hardly know the food had been there. Some of them would never eat anything, just look at the tray of food and then at me with a disdainful look, as if to say, 'I ain't eating that.' Some of the children I fed too much, and their parents would complain about the three or four pounds their child had put on and the staff would all be told not to give out any extra food or candy, ever. The red-haired boy in the bed space to the left of the kitchen was pleading with me to give him his dinner twenty minutes before anybody else got theirs. His voice was piercing and ricocheted everywhere.

My co-worker, Patrick, was always cutting his tongue licking the tin cans full of tomato sauce and noodles. You can't put those in the microwave, the tin cans, or there'll be lightning and electricity everywhere. Patrick hit some of the children sometimes, but only the ones he didn't like, which meant only the bad children, the children that are probably used to it.

Patrick liked Helena. Helena never fed the children and never watched them sleep. She cleaned up after them and made sure no one got any bruises or bloody noses in their play. Helena was thirty-eight and Patrick was thirty-one.

The children loved to run around and yell loudly, but nobody really liked it but them, so they learned to not like it as much. What they learned to like most was to sit on the floor and stare at the window, waiting for their parents to come and take them home. The ones that didn't go home by eight o'clock were disappointed and worried, and we'd tell them to go to sleep. Sometimes some children stayed overnight for three or four weeks. One of them for eighteen months.

The red-haired boy had learned to enjoy sitting under the table in the daycare room, which is what he usually did all day when he wasn't in his cage. When he was in his cage he didn't always act so docile and he'd often flip his food tray over and smear the food on the wall and floor, just to let us know he didn't like us.

The noodles and sauce tasted good right out of the can, though I always stained my shirts eating them.

'Why do you hate me?' asked the red-haired boy.

'Because I have to be around you.'

'Would you hate me if you were around me but didn't *have* to be around me?' the boy tilting his head and burrowing his chin in his hand.

'I would never be around you without force having been applied.'

'Then you hate me. All the time.'

'But only because I'm forced to be around you,' I said, red sauce dripping from my bottom lip and onto my shirt.

'I'm *hungry*.'

'You are not special.'

'But everyone is special,' the boy said earnestly.

'Not everyone.'

The boy opened his mouth, then paused a moment to consider and weigh the exchange. Sitting on the end of the mattress, which was studded with sheets and blankets that the children had learned to not disturb by never placing their bodies underneath the sheets or the blankets and never letting the sheets or the blankets leave the mattress, the boy said, 'If I saw you in the street and said 'Hi,' would you hate me then?'

'Probably.'

'Why?'

'I hate everyone,' I said.

'Why do you hate everyone?'

Patrick walked into the kitchen through the first door and it slammed shut behind him. He took the can out of my hand and drank the last of the sauce and ate the last meatball that I had been saving for myself.

'How's feedin? Anyone chunking up?'

'Helena says she could use your chunk to help with cleaning,' I said, motioning with a nod of my head towards Helena in the green daycare room.

Patrick punched me in the arm and it hurt a lot, but I'm good at faking it when it hurts and they didn't mean it to hurt or they shouldn't know that it hurt. I smiled at him as best I could as he looked at me in that mean way guys like Patrick do when you've said something to insult them even though they were not actually insulted, and you both knew it was a joke, but they still have to punch you just so you know that they will punch you.

Sunday mornings growing up I would sit in a chair in the church balcony, a chair on its own, apart from the pews. It was a small church, but tall enough. Chandeliers and candleabra hung from the ceiling, bronze arms holding electric lights made to look like real candles. My dad, the preacher, sometimes told in his sermon about how when he was a kid, and his dad was leading the service, he, my dad, would wonder if he was strong enough to hurl a hymnal book from one end of the room to the other. I sometimes wondered about this sitting in the balcony, but mostly I wondered if I could jump from the balcony and reach the arms of the chandeliers and candleabra. And grasp them, and hold on, and sway over the congregation. I imagined the old ladies and adult men with mustaches and wives and children below, and imagined falling onto them, my body splayed over the old wooden pews.

The cages were all divided by some kind of synthetic wood product, white and smooth and almost impossible to stain. The children tried staining it with food and feces and urine, but Helena just hauled out the bleach and the rags and it was forgotten. The cages on either side of the red-haired boy were empty, and I sat down in one and breathed deeply.

'Sometimes when someone hits my arm it feels flouncy,' the boy said.

'Do not speak. And do not make up words.'

'You suck at smiling,' the boy said, settling carefully onto the mattress and exhaling.

'I am excellent at forcing a smile.'

'Not fake smiles. All smiles. I've never seen you smile and I'm here every day. When someone makes a joke you don't laugh – even if it's really funny – you just pretend to laugh.'

'So all my smiles look fake?'

'Yeah,' he said.

Patrick called me over to the other side of the large daycare room, the immense muscles of his arm bulging in the air as he requested my attention with it, and I walked across the green floor to him.

'Were you talking with that red-headed one over there?' Patrick asked, gesturing across the room with his throbbingly large thumb. 'A sobbing menace, that one. Open that cage door and see if he doesn't address your bollocks.'

Patrick spoke in foreign accents even though he knew how miserable he was at them. Patrick knew that most everything he did was miserable, but was in no hurry to rearrange things.

'He goes for the hobbin?' I said. It's difficult to know, sometimes, if people are as uninterested in conversing with you as you are with them.

'Aye, he does, do ya,' Patrick said from the corner of his mouth.

Patrick was always talking like that. Like pirates or Welshmen or Arabs or something. He said he got most of his voices from television.

'He tells me I never smile,' I said to Patrick, motioning across the room towards the boy. 'That I suck at it.'

'Yeah. It's more like you're in China but you don't know how to speak Chinese,' Patrick said. 'You've never done it before. You don't know *how*.'

The red-headed boy had gone mad for the moment and forced his face flush up against the cage door and was howling inanely. It's always strange when the children talk. They think because they can understand when *you* speak that you can understand when *they* speak. It must be so frustrating for them. Patrick says he can understand what they want by how what they say *sounds,* but I don't think like he does. My idea is that if they don't know that they that can communicate with me, then maybe eventually they'll stop trying to, though they're persistent, these children.

....

Helena was thirty-eight and wore her hair in a bun. She sometimes used pencils and pens to hold the bun in place atop her head. She was skinny and wore long pants on her long legs, and her nose pointed prominently upward. Helena had two boys and a husband. Sometimes you saw her outside of here, on the street or in a store. When you saw her in her regular clothes she looked dangerous. Her regular clothes were leather biker coats and long, black boots and denim blue jeans. She smoked Light 100 cigarettes and Patrick thought she looked really sexy when she smoked. When he knew Helena was outside smoking he'd spy on her, to watch her doing it.

Nobody ever knew Helena. Who she was. Why she was what she was. Why didn't anybody find out?

Helena was mopping the daycare room's green floor. The floor smelled awful and I never, ever touched it with my skin. The children would pee on the floor whenever they wanted. They always ran out after hours in their cages and peed on everything. It made the floor feel sticky and sandpaper rough when you walked on it.

We mopped up the urine with large-headed mops that sat in buckets filled with water, bleach and a green cleanser. (The brand name cleanser had some exotic chemical in it that only children were allergic to, so we used the generic version, which worked just as well.) The floor was either sticky or slippery when it was freshly mopped, depending on how corroded it was from all the bleach and urine. Helena always made sure the water was changed often and the floor thoroughly sanitized, though with children no single space is ever safe from filth and no single inch of the room could ever be cleaned enough to be clean.

I always sang when I saw Helena. This old

song that I hadn't heard in fifteen years:

> *'Don't let me break your heart, Helena*
> *Don't give me presents and don't give praise*
> *You're gonna let me dig my very own grave,*
> *Helena.'*

Helena glanced at me and then looked back to the spot on the floor she was mopping.

'Growing a beard, Lincoln?' she asked, her tongue poking from the corner of her mouth in merriment. She did that sometimes, got all merry and jovial, and we couldn't ever tell why.

'I was thinking about it. How's it coming in?' scratching my gristly, pale chin.

'How long have you been growing it?' biting her lip, cheeks trembling.

I laughed, watching her be so merry. 'Eight days,' I told her, smirking.

'What?' she said, drawing it out in the way people do when what they really mean to say is, *What are you thinking about that I'm not privy to?*

'What?' I said, in that way I do when I know *What* but ask anyways, just to be sure they want to know *What*.

'What are you laughing at?'

'Nothing, Helena,' I said, still laughing, looking at the darker green on the floor in a patch that had just been mopped. The floor always looked darker when it was wet. Most things do, I think.

....

I walked over to the kitchen and started preparing the food again. The red-headed boy started whining as soon as he saw me walking back towards the kitchen. *I'm real glad,* I thought, *that I can't understand what he's saying.*

Patrick followed me to the kitchen and started throwing grains of rice at me from the enormous tub of it in the fridge.

'Patrick, I need at least two more cans of sauce,' I said, letting the rice bounce from my face and chest.

'Why?' he said, covering his left eye to center a bull's-eye that hit my shoulder and stuck there. 'It's Friday. Just use *agua*.'

'We're supposed to mix the rice with sauce on Fridays.'

'Since when, me matey?'

As I picked rice from my shirt, my forehead and hair were barraged and I bowed my head in defeat, which didn't stop him one iota.

'Since always, Patrick. Go get the sauce.'

'We don't have anymore. I'll have to visit the ole store-a-reeno.'

With my head bowed and eyes closed I heard Patrick jostle the lid onto, but not seal, the tub of rice and slide it back into the fridge. I heard him open the door to the stairs and I heard the door close. Then Patrick waited until he thought I was thinking, *There's no possible way Patrick would have the patience to hold out for this long.* Then two handfuls of rice spattered and splattered over my head like heavy rain.

....

Every day about a dozen sets of parents would come into the store and ask for a tour. Colin, the tall and blonde owner, told everyone to 'discourage potential problems,' which meant if they looked like they'd complain and make Colin's life more unpleasant then say all the wrong things so they'd take their kids and business somewhere else. Colin was very pleased to own a business that was so successful he could turn away clients. We all hated most of the children, but we hated every single one of the parents.

Earlier in the day I had given a tour to a jittery dad who'd asked a shocking amount of questions.

'So they're out there all day?' he asked as we gazed through the window into the daycare room.

'No, not really all day-'

'Is this the basement?' the man interrupted, having noticed we were in the basement, looking around to certify his surroundings, as though he hadn't just walked down the stairs with me.

'The children sleep from eight at night till seven in the morning and the rest of the day they're either out there or in their cages.'

'Cages?' the dad asked, incredulous.

'Well, you know, their cells, their private spaces away from the other children.'

'That child's urinating on the wall!' the dad said, wide-eyed and pointing to AJ, who had pushed his slacks and underpants down to his ankles and was peeing on the wall, making large swoops and circles with the stream, which was running off the wall and onto the floor, all around AJ's sneakers.

'Look! Why is he doing that?' the dad asked. 'Why is he- And that child's going number two!' the dad exclaimed, pointing to Cindy who was squatting in the middle of the room and humming a song to herself, bouncing her head to her own tune.

'Don't worry,' I said, 'Helena's out there,' gesturing to Helena who was standing ready a few feet from AJ with the mop. 'Helena's got it.'

'Why are they doing that?' he asked. 'That woman's just going to pick that up with her hand?' with an hysteric disgust on his face.

'Well,' I said, 'it's not all glitz and glamour down here in the daycare room. Sometimes we have to read to the children, and oftentimes listen to them talk, which, if you've ever been around a kid – and of course you have – well you know how they can talk.'

'With her hand,' the dad said weakly, staring terribly into the room.

'We also take the children outside twice a day,' I continued, leading him back up the stairs and to the front desk. 'We serve a variety of meals, though if your child is on a special diet you're welcome to bring in your own meals.'

'Hand,' the dad mumbled.

'Yes, well, have a good one. Here's our card.'

....

The red-headed boy was chewing at the bars of his cage, at the bottom, near the red-painted floor. Sometimes the children would chew on them so voraciously that a few of the bars were now bent at the bottom. It never got them anywhere, all that chewing, but neither did the howling and moaning and they hadn't stopped doing that either. Many of the cage's bars were bent in at waist-level, from where we had all kicked at the bars to scare the children into being quiet or if we were just mad at them or at something else. Helena gave you sour looks when you kicked the cages, as if to say, 'I understand, but they're children. They're only children.' Which is an unacceptable excuse, I think. Patrick, too.

Patrick had still not returned with the sauce, so I sat down on the mattress in the cage and rubbed my eyes, the flesh of my hand driving into the eyeball, squishing it into the socket. The red-headed boy peered over the wall between us, fingers slipping through the bars and gripping the wall. 'Do you have a headache?' he asked.

'No.'

'You know you're the only one that talks to us?'

'Shut up.'

'No, really. Helena doesn't, Patrick doesn't. Patrick talks to himself. He thinks we can't understand what he's saying, or even that he's talking.'

His mouth was behind the wall, his eyes peering over the top of it, so that his voice was echoy and sounded big like a teacher or government employee.

'How come you never give Emily sauce? Even on Fridays? She wanted me to ask you that.'

'She deserves no sauce!' I said, standing and pointing my arm into the air towards the ceiling, 'And no sauce shall she get! It is rice and water only for Emily, betrayer and aristocrat!'

'Who did she betray?' the red-headed boy asked, his tiny eyes peering up at my massive face.

'Her? That debutante? That bourgeois madame? Dozens, I'm sure! Dozens!'

'But who-'

'Dozens, I say!' I said.

I let myself out of the cage and went back into the kitchen. The red-headed boy immediately threw himself up against the bars of his cage and started howling and screeching like he was always doing. I slammed the kitchen door, which kept out about a third of the wailing - a large portion considering the immensity of the cacophony surrounding us.

Helena opened the door and gave me a look with pouty, pushed lips, as though to say, 'I know you like slamming the door on them, but they're just children.' She was always wearing blue jeans – we were all always wearing blue jeans, which deflected and disguised (without letting soak in) the filth of children crawling *all over* you better than slacks or trousers or sweatpants did. I had writing all over my jeans: words and transient line-designs and right-angles and half-circles and blotches of darkened, scribbled ink. Patrick was always talking about Helena in blue jeans. He told me that sometimes he would go to the bathroom outside of the kitchen and masturbate because of Helena in blue jeans, but I think he might have just been exaggerating to prove a point, which when you do nothing you say can ever mean as much as you'd like it to.

Sometimes I saw the ghosts of the children walking beside the children, and I wondered why the children even bothered to continue running or eating or whatever it was, because they were only ghosts, or would be only ghosts one day. They didn't seem affected by this reality.

'Food! My food! You just made it! I know my special food bag!' the red-headed boy screamed at me, though I pretended I couldn't hear him. Helena had slammed the second kitchen door behind her, to show me how it felt, though I thought it felt great and it hurt my feelings the way she had tried to hurt my feelings like that. Helena's so skinny, Patrick told me, you feel like you'd break her if you tried hard enough. In bed, he meant, though he didn't say because he figured I would know, which I did. Ever since he had said that to me, about breaking Helena, I couldn't stop thinking about Patrick picking her up and breaking her over his knee, the way you would a stick when you're a kid, though I know that's not the way Patrick would want to break Helena. It was very violent to me, this desire to break Helena in Patrick. But I don't think that Patrick thought of it that way.

'Your name's Lincoln, right? Like the President?' the red-headed boy asked me, taking advantage of the fact that Patrick was probably making his way back from buying the sauce as casual as he could, shopping for sunglasses and eating pizza pie, forcing me to the mattress again, to rub away the ache in my eyes.

'Just like the President,' I said.

'What-'

I walked back into the kitchen, slamming the door behind me.

....

Patrick got in trouble once for strangling one of the children. Helena saw him do it and she started crying when she saw Patrick strangling one of the children. Patrick stopped when he saw that Helena was crying. When Colin, the owner of the place, saw Helena crying he asked her why and she told him. Colin had a special meeting with Patrick in the back room with the door closed. No one could hear any shouting or anything, but when Patrick came out of the room he was red-eyed and left to take his lunch break. Colin was as jolly as ever. The child was staying for a few more weeks so there was time for the bruises to fade before his parents arrived for pick up.

Patrick really wanted to bed Helena and it drove him out of his mind to see her every day and not be able to. I didn't see what the big deal was about with Helena, especially since Patrick kind of hated her. He always started fights with Helena just to be able to talk to her passionately. Plus, he got to scream at her sometimes if she screamed at him, and he was usually real angry at her, though not for the reasons he was screaming about. It was usually fights about how much bleach to use or which children to feed first. Helena liked to do everything the way she had originally intended to do it. Other ideas couldn't be considered right or wrong; they were void because they weren't part of the intended plan.

I was planning on ordering two large coffees with cream from the bagel shop and sitting in the park on my break. I'd probably get one with sugar and drink it second, because I wouldn't know what I was missing on the first and then would know exactly what I'd been missing on the second. The cream would be thick, like when you can actually taste it, can feel it's color and complexion on your tongue. The first cup would be too hot to drink but I'd drink it real quick anyways. The second cup would be immaculate.

I sat back down on the mattress among the screaming children, who were clanging their metal water dishes all over the place. The mattresses were firm in small, random knots and soft like belly fat in all the gaps.

'You always work on Sunday morning, right?' the red-headed boy asked me.

'Yes.'

'Don't you go to church?'

'No.'

'Why? My mom says everyone should go to church.'

'Everyone should.'

'So why don't you?'

His terrible red hair poked over the wall of his cage and he laced his fingers through the bars, his eyes peering down at me.

'Huh?' he asked. 'Why don't you?'

'Why don't *you*? Why doesn't your mom take *you*?'

'My mom says church is no place for children.'

'It's the only place for them.'

'What do you mean?' he asked.

The far kitchen door slammed and we both looked over. Patrick came into the kitchen, showed me the cans of sauce by shaking them in the air, and then slammed them onto the counter-top. Then he walked back to the door and left the kitchen. The door made a loud sound behind him. It meant he was tired of watching Helena walk around all day and being attracted to her while she was not attracted to him.

'Why is church the only place for children?' the boy asked me.

'You know when a baby's crying during the service? And no one says anything or gets annoyed or makes faces or talks bad about it after the service? And how it's cute if a kid just runs loose in the middle of the sermon and just like streaks down the center aisle like they'd just punched their sister and were running away from her?'

The boy didn't say anything.

'I bit my tongue right open in the middle of Sunday service once, when I was one or two years old. My dad was the pastor of the church and they had to stop the service so he could drive me to the hospital.'

The boy, peering with big eyes, asked, 'What

happened?'

'I was laughing real hard and just bit my tongue down the middle is what they told me. In the hospital they gave me popsicles to numb my tongue and my Dad said that no matter the flavor or color of the popsicle, they all turned red from the blood in like twenty seconds.'

'So they just kept giving you more popsicles?'

'Yeah, they gave me two boxes, my dad said,' I said. 'He said I was laughing and enjoying the limitless popsicles.'

'What's limitless?' the boy asked.

'It's forever.'

'Like God?' the boy asked.

'Kind of.'

'Do you have a Bible? My mom says everyone should have a Bible in their house.'

'Yes,' I nodded.

'Do you read it?' he asked.

'Someone spilled something on it and all of the pages got wet,' I said.

I stood up and swung the cage door behind me. The boy threw himself up against the bars of the cage and began screaming. I opened the cans of sauce and started making the rest of the meals. Patrick entered the kitchen and slammed the door.

'You see that movie on cable last night?' Patrick asked, leaning up against the counter.

'No.'

'The one with the guy from *Goodfellas*.'

'Robert Deniro?' I offered.

'Yeah yeah,' Patrick said. 'And the guy from *Home Alone*.'

'*Casino*?'

'But what's the guy's name?'

'Is it the guy from *Casino*?' I asked Patrick.

'Yeah.'
'Was it *Casino*?'
'No, no,' he said.
'Was it *Raging Bull*?' I asked Patrick.
'No, no.' he said. 'But what's the guy's name?'
'Was it *Goodfellas*?' Patrick just stared at me. 'Funny how? How am I funny?' I lazily recited.
'Yeah yeah!' he said, emphatically.
'That's *Goodfellas*, Patrick.'
He leaned against the counter and started tossing rice into and at his open mouth. He exhaled heavily.

'It's not right,' he said and then paused. He was frustrated, Patrick. I could tell because it was the only time he didn't talk a lot of nonsense or goof around. 'It's unfair ... That she can.' He tossed more rice towards his face with his open mouth. 'Walk ... around ... like ...' and, instead of finishing his sentence, started gesturing wildly with his arms towards the daycare room, where Helena spent all of her time, mopping and scrubbing, separating the fighting children.

What I thought that Helena knew but she didn't know was that Patrick always fell for whoever worked in the daycare room. He had been here seven years, though in only two Helena had been able to best him as far as control of that room and the children and what all, and only because Patrick always fell for whoever was working the daycare room. I thought that he had pretty much given up on the hope of bedding Helena, but that didn't matter too much to the way he acted towards her. Patrick wanted to bed Helena but was instead trying to break her, though he'd give up that pursuit if she'd sleep with him.

'She's married. Has kids.'

Instead of responding vocally Patrick winced with his face and cringed with his body to signify that the thought of Helena in blue jeans was so sexy it was painful. I think a lot of Patrick's pains came from sex, though never where he'd expected them.

I thought about asking him if he was attracted to Helena's personality, which I though persnickety and distant. But I never asked him because I could only expect his honest affirmation of his attraction and I didn't think Patrick would have known what the question meant. Talking with Patrick about sex was like being really hungry and talking to someone who'd just been to a smorgasbord but was complaining about being hungry anyway.

Colin, the boss, opened the kitchen door and then the next one and then the door into the daycare room to retrieve his child, Kevin. Patrick and I tried to look like we were working intently so Colin would have no reason to think that we were not. We all doted on Kevin, at first because he was the boss's kid and you felt guilty if there was a child anywhere near you that you weren't doting on; but after a while you quit that and only fed the ones you liked and only gave blankets to the ones you liked, though Helena was pretty militant about the linen and stuff and sometimes you had to wait till she'd left for the night before snagging one of the children's bedding and putting it on the shelf high up above their heads. But Kevin was a nice child who you'd give some blankets to anyway, just because he kept quiet and was usually clean.

Patrick hadn't been able to find something to do that looked productive and Colin asked him, 'Hey, Patrick, is there something you could be doing?'

'He could be getting me more sauce,' I said, to ease the tension of being present when Colin scolded someone, 'and of the correct brand and size, maybe,' which was a dig on Patrick but saved him some potential verbal reaming from Colin, which was far worse.

'Patrick,' Colin invited with an outstretched arm, ushering him out the door and up the stairs, Kevin in tow.

The red-haired boy asked me what it had been like at school when I was a kid. I told him that I didn't think that I had learned anything, at least of the things they wanted us to learn. And that that kind of felt like a learning on its own, you know?

'And did you always want to work with kids?'
'I never wanted to work with kids.'
'Not even now?'
'Not even now.'
'Where did you go to school? In the city?'
'No. I am not from here. I am from away.'
'Where away?' He sneezed three times, rapidly.
'Upstate. Christian school.'
'My mom wants me to go to Christian school, just 'cause she says the teaching is better than regular school.'
'She's right. But it is awful in different ways.'
'What do you mean?'

I coughed and wished for a coffee maker in the kitchen, which gleamed silver.

'Children should be exposed to all kinds of harmful things so that their bodies can learn of them and from them, and grow defenses. The Christians try to keep these harmful things from you. But later, when you get exposed to the harmful things, you won't be able to defend yourself. You won't know what is happening, or what you can do about it.'

'You sound like you hated school,' the red-haired boy said.

    I shrugged. 'Like is awful. So go to the schools. They are awful. So go to the churches. They are awful. So go to the human beings. Who are awful.'

    'Then the only good that can be done will have to be done by the awful.'

    'Good luck.'

....

I once lost my brother's tow truck in the stream next to our parent's house. We were playing with our trucks on the shoddy wooden bridge in the far backyard. Our neighbor's granddad, Mr. Oster (who adored me), had built it when I was three years old and we had just moved from Connecticut to New York. I was always talking with Mr. Oster when he was working in his garage and he gave my parents an enormous television set because, 'Lincoln should be able to watch his cartoons in color,' my dad'd said he'd said. Until then we'd been watching all of our shows on a black and white set, which was maybe nine inches or so. Mr. Oster, on a different occasion, also gave my father a bag of candy so large that Dad just had to laugh at it, especially since Mr. Oster instructed my father that it was 'Only for Lincoln,' though we all ate the candy.

    The tow truck was big and blue and he'd just gotten it for his birthday which was the same day that I'd lost it. I never understood how it could possibly be that I had lost my brother's new truck the very day he had gotten it. If it were a story it's definitely what would've happened. It would have been the cliché, expected thing to have happened and I had never thought of myself, my existence, as cliché. But there I was looking under the bridge and soaking my jeans and socks and sneakers in the stream and stomping through the tall grass and little trees that sprung up on the banks. It was shiny and dark blue and had silver and chrome all over it. Big headlights. Huge tires with white writing on them.

    I had rolled it all the way across the width of the bridge, running low to the ground, and launched the truck off of the elevated board at the edge, in the direction of the house and the road in the distance. We looked on the other side of the bridge anyways, mostly because my brother, Isaiah, figured if I were fool enough to lose the truck I was probably too foolish to know where to find it. I searched the wrong side of the bridge with him anyway to make myself subservient because I wanted him to know I was sorry.

    Mr. Oster had also built the large barn all the way back, across the field and into the forest. It used to be used for pigs though they didn't do that anymore. I was afraid that if I went inside there'd be the ghosts of pigs and they'd be eating the ghosts of food out of the troughs. Isaiah always told me there weren't any pigs or ghosts in the barn, but I never went inside to see.

....

When you smoked with Helena outside on the street she would talk through the entire smoking of the cigarette. Since she punctuated every statement or question with a drag of the cigarette, they were smoked quickly, and I would have to be diligent with my own cigarette to keep pace.

    'You saw me,' she said, pursing her lips in an accusatory way. She already knew I was about to play dumb.

'Where?' I smiled.
'You know where, you.'
I shrugged, frowned.
'You know where. In your neighborhood. You saw me.'
'On Saturday?' I gave in, finally. 'I didn't know if it was you on that motorbike.'
'Yes you did, Mr. Lincoln.' Her 'yes' sounded like 'chyes.' 'Chyes you did. Why you didn't say Hello?'
'I wasn't sure it was you.'
She waved at me dismissively, dragging on her cigarette, as though there were no one in the world who would have believed me.
'You wear blue jeans everywhere,' I said.
'Chyes!' She was adamant. 'Here you must, for the children. And on a motorcycle...' Then she laughed, which sounded like a confirming 'Ah ho ha hoooo...'
'What do you think of God, Helena?' I did not want to talk about her being in my neighborhood on a motorcycle.
'I know God is up there,' she pointed to the sky, or to the scaffolding above us. 'And he love me and I love him.' She shrugged. 'And that is all.'
'What you think of Patrick, Helena?' I laughed, asking the question. She laughed and scolded me with a playful look and an accusatory finger pointing.
'You are try to get me going, Mr. Lincoln.'
'Patrick, he's the one, no?'
'He's the one to leave alone.' This sounded like 'alo.' 'He is the heart-breaker with no heart.'
I quoted a book I had recently read. 'Do you think blue jeans are the universal uniform, Helena?'

'Chyes!'

....

The red-headed boy had been laying on the mattress quietly for at least five minutes, but when he heard the kitchen door opening he threw himself up against the bars again and started to scream. I kicked the bars and screamed back at him and sat down in the adjacent cage.

'How long have you been here?' asked the boy.

'Two years.'

He peered over the wall at me sitting on the bed, arms draped over my kneecaps.

'When are you going to quit?'

'When I can.'

'My mom was listening to this book-tape with me about this guy who always loses and then at the end he wins.'

'We never win, child.'

'Sure we do,' he said, chirping it gurpbally.

'You may. We don't. We around you,' gesturing to the wholeness of the building.

I wished that Patrick would be back so I could finish with the meals and drink my coffee, the first without sugar, the second with. I also needed to be away from Helena, who looked so dynamite in blue jeans I'd fantasized about marrying her even though I didn't like her. She was a very negative person, Helena; or at least she made everyone around her negative.

'David Copperfield won,' the red-haired boy prodded.

'But he's fictitious and I'm not.'

'So, it's gonna be a little harder on you, then.'

Helena was so attractive to Patrick that she made all the women around her attractive to him as well, but unsatisfying. That's why Patrick was always having sex with all the other women, without much effort, he'd confided, and without caring whether it happened or not. Patrick was always still only looking at Helena in blue jeans in the green and disinfected daycare room.

'Um, so, lemme ask you a question,' the boy said. I waited silently. 'How come you always say that you can't understand what we're saying but are always talking to us anyway?'

'I'm not talking to you, red-haired boy. It has been said, or should have been, that when you talk to a child you are talking to yourself.'

'But I'm talking to you.'

'*I'm* talking to *you*,' I said.

'And I'm talking back to you,' he said.

'*I'm* talking back to *you*.'

....

Patrick returned with the sauce and then went to the bathroom. I finished making the meals and got into an argument with Helena about who would give them to the children. I agreed to do it when she put her hand on my arm, which was the first thing she did.

When I fed the children I would open the cage doors with my left foot up to block an escape and slide the food tray in on the floor real quick and then close the door and lock it. After a while the separate acts became one motion. The children were always trying to escape from the cages and lots of times you caught them between the wall and the closing cage door and had to force them back into the cage with your foot. We all used a broom to drag the trays and the water bowls through the slim crack of the open door when feeding time was over, blocking an escape with our bodies.

Helena helped me to drag out the empty food trays. I was going to get both coffees from the store a few streets away that had very large sized coffee cups, which I usually didn't go to because it was sixty cents more per cup, and the extra time spent walking meant less time in the park, though any time outside of the building was glory.

'Helena, Helena,' I sang. 'Helena, Helena.'

'Isn't the words to that song,' one of the children said and then sang, 'Corrina, Corrina,' snapping her fingers in time. 'Corrina, Corrina.'

I stared blankly at her.

'My dad has that on record,' the child said. 'And it's in this movie-'

I walked back out into the daycare room so I didn't have to talk to the children anymore. Helena was smirking as I passed her, but she kept her head down and continued sweeping all the spilled water towards the drain. Helena never laughed all that much, just smirked mildly or spoke loudly to signify excitement or importance.

On my way to the kitchen Patrick rushed by me towards Helena. They were about to have a fight and I didn't want to be close to it. They both knew some language I didn't and screamed at each other in it, which made the conflicts more frightening. When they fought Patrick looked as though he wanted to tear Helena's clothes off violently, and Helena looked like she didn't want to tear off Patrick's clothes.

They always moved when they were fighting: they didn't stop working, they just fought and helped each other at their tasks while they fought, which is why Colin never bothered to interfere, though he hated both of them anyway, I think, for other reasons.

I was in the kitchen washing my hands and arms in the sink when Helena rolled over an empty mop bucket to the spicket outside the kitchen window. Patrick walked alongside her carrying the mop and the squeegee for the bucket.

'You cannot feed CJ everyone else's food just cause they don't eat it!' Patrick said.

'He was still hungry,' Helena said, watching with a careful eye to see how much bleach Patrick was putting into the bucket.

'He weighs a hundred pounds and he's seven!'

'You don't know what it's like to be hungry!'

'I'm always hungry!' Patrick said. He was always saying stuff during their arguments that didn't mean anything or was entirely inane to the subject, which is another reason why he usually lost. Most of what Helena said was practical.

'Too much bleach,' Helena pouted in warning.

Patrick kept pouring it in. Helena grabbed the bucket handle and rolled the bucket away from him. Patrick followed, running in squatting position across the daycare room floor, pouring the bleach into the moving bucket.

'Stop! You creep!' Helena said, having reached the far wall.

'I'm always hungry!' Patrick screamed at her.

Patrick did not stop (I assumed he was going to pour the entire gallon of bleach in, causing the bucket to overflow, which he'd have to mop up) and Helena kept screaming what were probably curse words at him, though it was in that other language so

I wasn't sure what she was saying, only that she looked angry and was screaming. When the bottle was almost empty Helena bent over and tipped the bucket into Patrick, dowsing his legs and feet.

'You're bald!' Helena screamed at Patrick, who continued to empty the last of the bleach onto the overturned bucket, splashing it onto both of them, though Patrick was not bald.

'I'm always hungry!' Patrick screamed at her.

'You're bald!' Helena yelled back. 'You're bald! You're bald! You're bald!'

Helena grabbed the bottle of bleach from Patrick and hit him in the head with it. That's why Colin had to fire her instead of Patrick, even though he liked Helena more. We chatted about it over coffee the next time I filled in at the front desk for a sick Manager.

The red-headed boy jumped up and down in his cage when he saw me carrying his food tray towards him, and spilled his water all over the floor. He ate the food so fast you couldn't even believe it had been there. Then he vomited and before I could clean it up Colin saw it and told me to give the boy a bath.

I soaked the boy with the hose as he stood in the large elevated tub, made of steel. I squirted shampoo and conditioner at him in giant globs and told him to scrub. The children hated baths and the smart ones learned that it was over much more quickly if they went along with it, plus we didn't curse at them as much. As I was using an enormous beach towel to help the boy dry himself off I inched my hands around his throat and began to cautiously throttle him. I shook him and his head wobbled loosely but the boy did not complain aloud, only with his eyes.

'See, you're smiling now,' the boy said. 'That's how you do it! That's how!'

43

Ona MOVE

Come. Step lively.

This is the cemetery I was telling you about, to your right. It looks like a park, I know, but if we were to climb yon hill (and we will be climbing yon hill) we would meet the gravestones about halfway up, behind the evergreens. At the top of the hill, where Highland Avenue South ends and urges traffic left or right, onto Highland Street: up there we would find the large mausoleum where the neighborhood kids congregate, come nightfall. I see them evenings when I walk to the corner to use the payphone, see them sitting on the mausoleum full of remains of people whose names are street names and county names, more than they are names of people who once could climb hills and make names.

My roommate, Manfred, says there are police barricades all around the neighborhood. He says that he can't get to us from work; to the apartment. I called him an hour ago for a favor while he was at work, and he said he'd tried to come home earlier but the police had barricaded the streets in a rectangle that included our apartment. He's still driving that VW his dad fixed up and gave to him. Yeah, Ramona, I'm still driving the Lumina I bought with a loan the credit union gave my dad.

And this was at noontime that Manfred couldn't get through to the apartment. Over two hours ago. You're right, Ramona, must be to do with the house on Osage Avenue, where there is always trouble going on. Those people killed a cop when they lived in a different neighborhood a few years ago. Nine of them went to jail for killing that cop, Officer Ramp. They would not even defend themselves in court, I remember; they didn't recognize the authority of the court. And now at their house at 6221 Osage Avenue they're always screaming out of megaphones, megaphones that they rigged up into the trees in front of the house. Always screaming, 'Motherfuck this and motherfuck that. Systems this and oppressions that.' I know it's only a few blocks from my apartment on Highland, but I am ecstatic not to live on Osage. Not that I've ever said anything to anyone about it, except to Glassey maybe, this guy I know in the neighborhood, who hopefully we won't be meeting.

They call these 'the cuts,' Ramona, where we are walking now. 'The cuts.' The spaces between the houses and along alleys to other alleys. I learned the term just recently at work at the convenience store, from a coworker, Jeff. Obviously it derives from 'short cuts.' But Jeff is from the sticks of Lafayette, so don't take it too seriously. Although Jeff was the one who brought me to Osage in the first place, to make the acquaintance of Doug the Nug, the man who is always holding. That's another slang term I'm using for your benefit, Ramona. Taking you into my confidence, Ramona. Holding substance; holding contraband. In possession of.

'Manfred, hey.'

'Hey Jonah what's up.'

'Sorry for the second call today while you're working-'

'No problem what's up?'

'I'm with Ramona. Near Osage. What's going on?'

'Go inside and watch TV, Jonah. It's all over the TV. There's a blockade, the cops are telling everyone to get out. If you were at home they would have told you first hand.'

I rarely come here, Ramona, to Osage

Avenue. Where is there to go? There is the first street-corner where I first saw a sex-worker. And the wholesale depot where Manfred purchases quantities of beers and liquors. And streets so dangerous the loiterers steal your tires even while you're driving the car, is the old joke. And that old woman on the porch grimacing.

That man approaching us, that's Glassey. I know him from coming here to see the man Jeff told me about. He is good, Glassey. He is familiar. He spends all day cutting the cuts. All night, as well. You see him around when you've cuts to be cutting, when you're cutting the cuts. He talks like that. He will nod. Nod back. Try to say nothing, even if spoken to. Not because he is dangerous, but because he will never shut up.

'Hey, Jonah, man.'

'Ramona, this is Glassey. Glassey, Ramona.'

'Hi, Ramona, nice to meet you what the fuck is going on here, Jonah?'

'I don't fucking know at all.'

'They want us to leave. To *vacate*.'

'Now?'

'Yeah. Now. The whole neighborhood. Bunch of cops going around, telling everyone to leave for twenty-four hours. Why should I leave? This wasn't declared a disaster area. I don't see any reason to leave, unless they're planning to blow up everything around here.'

'Not in the daytime, Glassey.'

'Oh yes, in the daytime, Jonah. Down here on Osage they don't have the decency to die at night. They die here at midday. That's the Osage secret. . . Ah, Jonah, just cross your fingers and use up all of your wishes. And don't look for Doug the Nug, neither, he ain't holding and he ain't even in the *county* anymore after the cops knocked on *his* door. And pretty soon they gonna be knocking down the Osage door. That's right, Jonah. 6221 Osage is having it once and for all. And don't they deserve it, throwing their garbage everywhere 'cause they believe in recycling or some shit. And attracting rats and roaches and they got a hundred dogs and a hundred cats, Jonah, don't you know it? And hollering bullshit out of the trees all day and night at folks. That crew is gone get it, Jonah, and you know 'cause *I* told you so, and you know I know the inside of it, Jonah. You know what I'd do, Jonah? I'd tell them they got so many minutes. And if they didn't come out, I'd level the place, kids and all. You don't want to leave any kids growing up wanting vengeance.'

You can wave to Glassey as he leaves, Ramona, but he never waves back.

And what now? To my apartment on Highland? I don't have much I would want to take from there. I don't want to take anything with me. I don't want to go. Why should we go? Are they planning to nuke the place or something? You know, there is an attic in my apartment. It's kind of a sleepy place.

....

Sorry, I almost fell asleep there, Ramona. It's past midnight already. I can't believe I'm not hungry. I told you the attic was a sleepy place.

I know, I too can't believe that the house at 6221 Osage Avenue has not made a sound. I know. They're usually 'motherfucking this and motherfucking that' all over the place. Telling everybody everything that's wrong and so on. And now the cops empty the neighborhood, and 6221 is staring down how many cops out there? And fire trucks? And how many fire-fighters? And they don't make a *sound*?

Oh! How on cue was that blast of feedback from the trees, Ramona? Painful dispatches in blasts from megaphones in the trees. I think it is the sound of crying babies. Yeah, crying babies in the house on Osage.

'You're going to see something you've never seen before.' It sounds so dominant and terrifying coming from those megaphones. Must be a man speaking. 'Send in the CIA. Send in the FBI. Send in the SWAT teams. We have something for all of you.' What the hell are they talking about, Ramona? Yes, I'd be scared if two-hundred cops and fire-fighters were hanging out outside my house, waiting for me. Yeah, I'd try to escape somehow. No, I know I'm not a cartoon, Ramona, but I don't know... I know I can't dig a tunnel to China, yes, Ramona, I know.

That's the police commissioner right there. Are you hungry? I wish we had something intoxicating to consume so that we could settle down into disorientation. Although I know you don't ingest intoxicants, even in jest. But for some, disoriented takes the cake. It is what one is doing.

I think I'm getting splinters in my fingers from leaning my hands onto this beam to look out the window. Who is that guy, passing on the street below? Is he familiar to you? Not to me. He walks quickly and with great purpose. If I were passing him on the street, I would not look at him; but I definitely would not *not* look at him. You see guys like that all the time, Ramona, I know.

Goddamnit, they must've cut the power. Is it out across the street? Yes. And down the block? Yes.

But the streetlight is still on. And there is just nobody out there, Ramona. Everyone else is gone. And the streetlight just flashed a brilliant flash before it too dissolved and left the neighborhood illuminated only by the enormous electric-light apparatuses muscled in by the authorities, on Osage, below; and all of the headlights of their red and blue motor vehicles.

....

I'm sorry, Ramona, I fell asleep. Just for a little bit. Did you? No. What's been going on? I need to pee. Where's the bucket?

     Remember that girl named Dottie? She lived with Doug the Nug, the man who Jeff introduced me to who was always holding. Yeah, the Doug that Glassey said has deserted the neighborhood like it was on fire. Remember Dottie, with the missing front tooth that nobody ever noticed? She's got her other teeth in abundance, anyway. And her dog, Puppetino, who always lay in the doorway of the house, and you had to make friends with him before you could step over him and follow Dottie to speak with Doug. There were always treats on the counter-top above Puppetino that Dottie would leave for visitors' use. And you'd have to hold a treat and let Puppetino smell your hand, palm down in a fist in case he decided to bite. Then the cookie, palm up. You had to let him lap his tongue to your skin; his soft Molossus' jowls. And then you step, step over, and follow Dottie through the kitchen, beyond the running faucet dashing water into the piles of plates yellow with egg-yoke and tiny food crusts, brown and gray with sundries, splashing water becoming puddles on the counter-top. And Doug, in the recliner in the den Dottie led us to. (I know not *us*,

Ramona, not me and *you*, Ramona. *Us* meaning *me*; and whoever I was with.) And Doug the Nug in that green bathrobe, ketchup and mayonnaise on the collar. Cheese slices poking from the pocket. He would never remember a name. He skirts the issue of names by using 'Dude' or 'Man,' or in how he snaps his fingers or bangs an object to get my attention, instead of just calling my name.

It is light out there, Ramona. Thanks for making me take notice. I might have nodded off again. Holy shit that is a lot of cops. That is a lot of fire-fighters. Holy fucking shit Ramona Ramona. I don't know weapons very well, Ramona. Tell me what you see. A water cannon, okay. Browning rifles? M-50s *and* 60s? *Uzis*? I didn't even know Uzis existed outside of like Mogadishu and Herzegovina. And what else? You think you see an anti-tank gun? Holy crow, Ramona, does the house at 6221 Osage Avenue have a tank? Is that an eviction notice the police commissioner is serving 6221? What a motherfucker.

Can't they just use an armored car and ram down the doors, Ramona?

And now the trees at 6221 are talking again, saying,

'This ain't gonna be no goddamn repeat of your history. We're gonna give you motherfuckers a taste of something different. You gonna get the best. This ain't gonna be no goddamn Grenada.'

And remember, Ramona, Doug would find any girl I was with to be beautiful. And his bookshelves full of books from school bookstores, which Doug liked the sight of, the books.

And remember- No, I know, Ramona, they just turned the water cannon onto 6221, the water cannon that can shoot a couple thousand gallons in a minute. Where'd they get all that water from? I know it's not playing games anymore, Ramona, I know. And I know that was shots fired just now. I think the police are firing at the house. Is the house firing back? Is it? The trees are saying, 'We ain't got a motherfucking thing to lose, so come on down and get us.' But they just keep shooting for five minutes. Ten minutes. Twenty. Forty. They'd better send to the police academy for more bullets, Ramona, wouldn't you think? What have they got going on down there that they need to shoot so much? Is 6221 bringing out a tank?

The cops stopped shooting. Nothing coming from the house. The trees are screaming with crying babies.

More shooting. More shooting than I thought could get done in a day. And that's tear-gas they're shooting into the house now? They just blew holes into both sides of 6221, near the front porch. How did they do that?

We'd better be *real* careful, as it's getting very light out now. There's sharpshooters on all the roofs, I think. Let's hope they're only shooting at 6221.

....

Sorry I fell asleep again, Ramona. I'm like the disciples in Gethsemane. When the shooting stopped I just about collapsed from the release of tension. It's forty minutes until noon. The water cannon has even stopped! They probably shot half-a-million gallons at the place. It's quiet enough to wake the dead. You don't think that's clever, Ramona?

The trees are saying,
'Testing, murderers, testing. You're trying to

kill breastfeeding mothers and breastfeeding children. We're not backing down. If you want us out, you'll have to bring us out dead. We are hearty and healthy. Tell the world you killed black babies for a health violation.'

    The trees are saying,

'The gate is open. Stop playing games. What are you killers waiting for? Our door is wide open. Your pictures will be plastered everywhere. Is your insurance paid up? Your wives will cash it tonight.'

    The trees are saying,

'I was talking with my sister, Rhonda, and I said, "They blew half the porch away." And Rhonda, she was just laughing, laughing.'

....

But come, Ramona, step lightly. I dreamt about midday on Osage Avenue, after leaving Doug and Dottie behind. Stepping over Puppetino, the dog. Watching the only sprinkler on the block water the only lawn. Seeing the girls so pretty they must have trains waiting at stations. The cat-calls of footsteps. Toys on lawns, broken, as useful as rocks. Balls that won't bounce, nets that won't catch. And the sunlight seeks us, shows us off as we smile and validate the avenue we are leaving behind.

    Oh God bless you, Ramona, you found my shitty old attic radio. And there's batteries. *Extremely low volume.* Is that the Mayor? That is the Mayor, saying,

'We intend to take control of the Osage Avenue house by any means necessary. I am totally convinced the group is bent on violent confrontation, and so are- That is, I don't believe there is any way to extradite them without an armed confrontation.'

The Mayor is saying,

'They have heavy artillery. They have tunnels dug under the neighborhood. There have been thousands of rounds fired. I have had their neighbors calling my office for months and even years complaining about 6221 Osage Avenue. What we want to avoid is the worst that could happen: the loss of property.'

The Mayor is saying,

'From here on my back porch three miles from Osage Avenue, I am taking full responsibility for this confrontation. I pray to God Almighty the children will not be hurt.'

You say that's Rhonda's mother down there with the cops, on the sidewalk, about half-a-block from 6221? She's shouting through a megaphone, to Rhonda, I guess. No fucking way Rhonda can see her from that angle. I wonder if they can hear her over that water cannon.

Is that the police commissioner on the radio? Saying we cannot tolerate this resistance to official power? Saying he's gonna make Attila the Hun look like a faggot by the time this is over? I dunno, some German guy, I guess.

....

I hate the sound of helicopters, Ramona. God, I hate helicopters. And look who I'm talking to, right? They brought a helicopter out to your Powelton Village house, no? So many years back? Yeah.

In my dream we are well away from Dottie and Doug's house, and all ways are clear to cross all streets. To the park. The thick grass. Then the gravestones, up yon hill. We can almost see it, my apartment. And I am telling you about New England, where my parents were born in towns so small they might not exist anymore. And I am telling you about the hills where no one makes a sound, and I tell you we will get blessedly lost out there, somewhere in the summertime, up on the mountains, naming all the hamlets, hurling stones down the sides and trying to break large strewn branches below.

And the helicopter is flying over the houses on Osage. And over 6221. It's getting dark out there. And what's that? They're just hovering over 6221. That guy leaning out of the helicopter, he's swinging something, looks like a bag, one of those canvas backpacks like you have. And where's the helicopter going off to now? Just racing away like they stole it.

Find another radio station, Ramona, see if there's any new stuff about the helicopter. If we had a television up here maybe they'd know.

And in my dream we were singing, Ramona, singing,

> *My grandma and your grandma*
> *Sitting by the fire.*
> *My grandma told your grandma,*
> *'I'm gonna set your flag on fire.'*

Jesus Christ what the hell was that? An explosion for certain. At 6221. The whole fucking roof is on fire. Jesus, did they light the house on fire, Ramona? Didn't you find anything on the radio?

....

The man on the radio is saying they dropped four-and-a-half pounds of Tovex and C-4 onto the roof of 6221. Is that a lot? Anything is a lot for a house, I guess, right? God, it was just, like it bust like, and it would be all like break stuff up. An enormous and blinding body of fire stretching twenty-five feet into the air. Scattering debris.

Black and white smoke. Black smoke. Great quantities of black smoke coming from 6221. It is over for the roof. Where the hell is the water cannon? I *told* you they would run out of water. The flames must be thirty-feet high. And the smoke is as black as you, Ramona, and you always prided yourself on being the blackest. Ha ha, I know, I know it's serious, Ramona, I know. And the flames are almost fifty-feet high, Ramona. And what is it that 6221 wants that they won't surrender? I mean, *I* wouldn't come out either if I was in there, but. . .

Oh right, yeah, the nine brothers and sisters that killed that cop? Okay, that were *framed* for killing that cop, Officer Ramp? So if those nine are released from jail this would be over? I know it's too late for *over*, Ramona, I know. And the flames must be seventy feet high, Ramona. Maybe eighty. And the smoke is black enough to wash coal with. Don't you think that's clever, Ramona? And the flames must be a hundred-feet high by now, Ramona. Taller than the house itself.

Finally, the water cannon revives. I've seen so many movies of fire-fighters saving people in a burning house. How are they going to reconcile this with the police, who are hesitant to stop firing at the burning house? On the radio the fire marshal is saying they are fire-fighters, not infantryman. But that doesn't sound like any fire-fighter I know, and I grew up right next to a fire station.

And the front of the house just fell into the house, Ramona. The front of the house just fell into the house. And there's some more shooting, I can hear. Coming from the back of 6221. In the cuts.

Is that 6221 shouting something? I think they're shouting something. Yeah, they're shouting, 'The kids are coming out! The kids are coming out!' In the back of the house they are trying to come out, but the cops are afraid of getting shot so they are shooting.

That's a kid that's climbing the fence in the cuts, near the front of 6221. There's flames and debris everywhere. Didn't 6221 have like twenty dogs and twenty cats? They got that kid, see, the cops got that kid, Ramona. They're dragging him away from there. And there's a woman, in the alley, trying to get away from the house. She is as black as nighttime? Yeah. And looks burned up. They got her, too, Ramona, they're searching her for weapons.

And the fire is everywhere, Ramona. All over the block. On the radio the man is saying the fire is at four alarms. They're summoning extra equipment. If only they hadn't run out of water before, when it was just a little fire on one house. On the radio the mayor is taking full responsibility for the war. And the fire has gone to five alarms. And the trees aren't talking anymore. And all those houses, Ramona. They're all as bright as the sun at midday. And the fire has gone to six alarms. What are alarms, Ramona? That must be about sixty houses on fire on the block. And the flames are so inexpressibly beautiful. Like you, Ramona.

And do you think they'll raze this house like they razed the Powelton Village house, Ramona? And that woman they arrested, Ramona, they're charging her with assault, Ramona, and riot and resisting arrest. And here it is National Police Week, Ramona.

How do you think she felt, Ramona, assaulting those police? Did she do the righteous thing? Is there any measure to what righteousness is worth, Ramona? I told you this attic was a sleepy place.

Sophia Sara Bednarczyk

An old man with a silver walker was refusing seats on the bus. He casually and politely declined the offer of a vacant seat from a middle-aged woman with a wave of his arms in the air: bony and flabby, wrinkly puppy-pig skin.

Beside and around the bus numerous vehicles of various colors loitered and cluttered and vacated the narrow, bumpy streets in the late and warm afternoon. The sidewalks, also, were filled with people in the overwhelmingly Polish neighborhood. The thickly polluted smell of Newtown Creek snuck into the bus at each stop, and was quickly eviscerated by the bus' powerful air conditioning, which was loud. I looked at and admired the hard and beautiful faces of the Polish women in the bus and on the street, whose noses pointed proudly upwards, not straight. Most of them wore their hair short; and their legs long.

I had never been to Greenpoint until one week ago, when I'd moved to the Brooklyn neighborhood from a rotten apartment building on 155th Street, on the border between Washington Heights and Harlem. Leaving felt liberating; felt like being a refugee going from a bad place to a not as bad place.

The old man, Amittai, shuffled down the aisle several paces, pushing the silver walker before him. The sound of the walker sliding over the floor was like what I imagined a sandstorm would sound like: whish, whish. He was making room for the line of arriving passengers at the McGuinness Boulevard stop. He had written a short story when he was twenty-eight years old, and had mailed it to several people.

The bus' driver was working a double-shift, and had just come on duty forty minutes before. Amittai met my eye and smiled, opening his mouth as though to speak. I thought to make the effort to appear as though I were about to stand and relinquish my seat to him. Before I could even plant my feet in preparation to rise, he waved away my polite attempt at a gesture.

McGuinness was the only avenue in the neighborhood that was wide enough to merit a median, on which I had stood and suffered traffic, warily eyeing the bouquets of flowers taped to a pole emerging from the median. They mourned accidents I had not witnessed, and forewarned of more.

I thought about how I would like to comb the dog's plentiful fur once I was arrived home. And how Sophia had written her name on my only work-pants with ink, no less than seven times. And that I was not hungry, though just an hour prior, leaving my shift at a dog kennel in Manhattan, I would have done wicked things for something to eat.

Mom never said anything discouraging to others, which was in large part how she had accomplished the difficult task of being full up of grace.

Amittai refused the second vacant seat thirty seconds after declining the first - and mine - when a young black woman passed him, and spotted the same vacant seat offered him before. 'No no no,' he said, 'you sit, you sit. I can stand,' waving away the offer, his arm's flaccid skin flapping, soft as old breasts; bones brittle like elegant dishware or keepsakes. With one hand he casually held the high handrail, with the other he gripped the gray rubber of the walker.

Beneath a green awning reading 'Polska' in

white, curvaceous letters stood Sophia, in a green shirt and blue jeans. Nobody but other Poles ever pronounced her name correctly. Sophia Sara Bednarczyk. I had met her only one week ago.

Her shirt was long in the front and back, but curved mightily on the sides, allowing her midriff to be hugged and revealed. Amittai, Sophia's uncle, caught my eye in the mirror above the bus driver, and winked.

Sophia was waiting for the cigarette she held between two fingers to burn out, and was thinking about letters from soldiers. Not the sort of letters she had seen and heard in movies, which were always too short or overt. Later, at night, she was to meet two old friends and go dancing. She stood, smoking, hoping it would be the last time she saw them, and the last time she went dancing. Afterwards she was to meet me. I would ask her why she wanted to stop seeing her old friends, and stop dancing. She would explain again what she had found in her uncle's desk drawer.

Of all the instances and places that Sophia had scribed her handle onto my only blue jeans, just one remained (thanks to the washing machine at the dog kennel, used after each shift) on the right thigh. I wished that they all would remain, making me a marked man for the first time in my life of letters and imaginary loves. I was not hoping to make a career of dog kennels, to be sure.

I was thirsty, though did not want to drink anything. I imagined the sugar-red of cranberry juice, the light brown of homemade iced tea, and the sweet sick flavor of diner chocolate milk, though I did not want to curb my thirst. There was something satisfying about being thirsty.

The next stop, Kingsland Avenue, emptied a

half-dozen seats onto the sidewalk as the passengers made their way home, or into the pizza parlor on Nassau Avenue; or into the general store. Amittai sat down, combing his stone-gray hair with his long fingers sliding through it, left to right. The name of his perfect and only story had been 'Freshness Is All,' though he reverted to its original working title of 'Snowden' when it was not published; and later never gave thought to the title again.

It was clear that summer was dying, though it was still too humid and heavy for the dog's fur-insulated comfort. I imagined him, Pressler, the dog, panting open-mouthed, sprawled on the kitchen floor in rectangular boxes of sunlight that shone through the back windows of the apartment. The young woman who had offered Amittai the seat had her hair styled in what girls called 'permanents' or 'perms.' It was a style popular when I was in elementary school, almost two decades ago. I wondered again what it might be like to bite into the silver handrail above me, the smooth metal on my tongue; my teeth sinking into it, itching the gums.

The man seated behind me looked thirty-six, but was twenty-nine. He wore a blue T-shirt which his wife had bought for three dollars at the local used-clothing store in the neighborhood next to Greenpoint, where all the French and other European elite children were moving in, after the place had been turned into a young bourgeois paradise. He was seething with anger, though he did not know why; or even that he was. Amittai winked at me and I briefly, discreetly, chuckled.

The bus driver kept the doors open at the red light on Kingsland, though it was not an official stop. A few passengers boarded the mostly empty bus, which was almost finished with its route.

Sophia had found her uncle's short story in his study, secretly, in the deep drawers inside the dark swirling black and brown desk. After she found the story she decided never to fall in love. With another person, at least.

Inside the Polska the cashier was giving a customer $0.05 less change than they were due. He made almost twenty dollars each week in this way. A teenage girl visiting friends from home in Connecticut perused the beverage aisle in the back of the store, contemplating the caffeine affects of one soda to the taste of another.

Outside the Polska Sophia stood, waiting on her cigarette and the end of her smoke break, before returning inside and running the cash register. She stared across the street into the light reflecting from the windows on the storefronts opposite. A passing man turned his head as he strode by her, to allow himself to appreciate her more completely. He pursed his lips in an expression that seemed to say, '*Damn*, it is just downright *ridiculous* that she would bring that out on the street and distract me with it while I am trying to get through the business of my day. But I appreciate it nonetheless.' Sophia saw him leering, and said something dismissive in Polish. He did not stop for a translation.

I read Amittai's story one week ago, when he had fallen asleep after dinner and Sophia snuck it from the study and presented it to me. I too hope to make the decision to never fall in love. I am not sure if Sophia will help or hinder this decision.

'Speak plainly, son,' Amittai called to me in the emptying and sunlit bus, none of the other passengers even looking up to see what he was shouting about.

Outside the Polska one week ago I had found

the story on Sophia's lips, when she asked me for a cigarette as I passed, and I met her for the first time. She had the story, she said, a story maybe like I wanted to write, she said. She had the story safe, in a deep drawer, in a dark, swirling, black and brown desk, underneath everything, in a deep and dark drawer.

It Was Me

If I could have written a letter that morning – while maintaining my balance – it would have been to the person who provided the majority of the body odor on the J train into Manhattan. I had earlier given a dollar to two musicians performing on the platform who were playing clarinet and bass guitar: caper music, no danger there. I, standing in the train, was staring at the city as we crossed the East River. The train's tracks several feet higher than the adjacent motor vehicles on each side. I felt a kinship with those driving into the city and to work, though I was not; and a longing and jealous loathing for those returning to Brooklyn, and rest.

Two girls across the aisle talked and laughed as one of them reached her arm all the way inside the tube of chips they'd been eating from to get at the last hidden bits. I formed and confirmed a personal judgment of the attractive woman sitting nearby, smiling and mooning over a used copy of *Lady Chatterley's Lover*. She laughs, I thought, not because it tickles her funny but because she wants someone (us?) to think she is sophisticated. I also considered whether she were reading at all. I was wicked.

I had helped my girlfriend Marcenda to bury her dog Bolivar near Newtown Creek, the dirt wet with petroleum. Then I had visited the Greenpoint Savings Bank. Part of the charm of my financial situation was that I would not know for five business days if I had beat Mrs. Kurska, the landlord, with my deposit or not. Marcenda, with nowhere to go and a heavy heart, followed me to the bank and then onto the J train, where I found her a free seat and, slowly, inched away.

The train moved lackadaisically over the bridge, as though afraid to tempt the supports with too much rattling about. In the center of a small wooden platform below the traffic I saw a bouquet where Eveline had seen a woman place a bouquet amidst the construction equipment; and then jump from the platform. If anyone else in the city had seen it happen Eveline was not aware of it, including even the *Times*.

I didn't know where the person who was supplying the greater amount of body odor was sitting or standing. I casually directed my attention, in hopes of spotting obvious suspects, beyond the confines of the novel I held before my face. I wondered if in Dreamtime we wouldn't have body odor, or at least we would be immune to it. I didn't think *Lady Chatterley* had been a very funny book, however lovely and desolate. What was attractive and alluring about Eveline, I had thought to tell Victoria earlier but hadn't, was that she wanted a world where objects and words *did* have a magical and potent significance. In Dreamtime the past existed within the present. Then how would I ever lose weight?

I wondered if we'd all be homeless and starving in a world where the subway car didn't have wall to wall advertisements.

With my nose behind my book, I could distinctly smell the divine,

Of the magically and potently significant: I, nose behind new pages, could unspeakable fragrance often worn by Eveline. It was beneath the potent, organic and significant body odor. I loved whichever female was wearing the smell, and longed for her to see me.

If I had a second letter to write it would have

begun, 'Dear MTA, Please stop broadcasting announcements in the subway cars. I know, with certainty, that of the five announcements made since the J train came to a standstill on top of the Williamsburg Bridge that nobody, myself included, understood a word of any of them. As sound pollution they are akin to those fellows who walk around the city playing loud music on large stereos. In this case, in my unhappy analogy, the fellows are blasting ear-aching fuzz with intermittent squawks and squeals which we cannot cross the street to escape from,' and so on.

We're transferring to other trains, I thought, as I did so at the City Hall stop. We're going onwards, limp and lame.

The handrail on the Uptown 6 train was hot from so many hands, the aisle crowded and nobody but those who'd been on since Canal Street sitting. I had happily pocketed the brief novel, *Walter, Waker, Boo Boo & Buddy*, before leaving the apartment that morning and could only barely hold it far enough away to read. A flash from the third rail sent me into shivers. Between Lockheed Smartin and some other fellows there were over 4,000 surveillance cameras in the New York City transit system. I shuddered again.

The most irritating consequence of the unintelligible announcements was how we all strained to hear them. Everyone hushed up a moment, while recoiling from them also straining towards them, the announcements, wanting to glean a word or phrase, fearful that this announcement could be the announcement that effected the way they traveled. I pondered my letter to the MTA and the commuting routines of MTA administrators, and if they themselves had ever attempted to *listen* to an

announcement on the subway train.
    Months later I received a letter, my address written in an elegant cursive, the envelope addressed to Senor Jonah Jeffries. It began, 'To gringo who bring the worst foul odor on J train. . . .'

Jesus' Teeth

Just as morning passed into afternoon Bethany, sitting on the toilet seat cover, removed all of her teeth for a cleaning. 'If my teeth are rotting,' she thought, thinking ahead to tomorrow's Easter Sunrise Service, 'then so are Jesus Christ's.'

Her fingers, small and delicate, pinched each tooth in turn with thumb and forefinger, pulling them loose. It felt like how she imagined a man felt when extracting himself after coitus. Bethany was only thirteen years old and had not even touched tongues with a boy, and thinking about coitus was like thinking about what it was like to live in Moscow.

The toilet lid was cold on her bare thighs and she waited for it to warm while removing her top teeth first, aligning them with precision on the sink's rim to avert mishaps for when she would later replace them. Out went the bottom teeth, too.

Pulling the final molar from its mooring she heard the far away sound of a million wind chimes being thrashed and thought she was passing out and gripped the sink-ledge with her free hand. Drawing the molar from her mouth she saw, trailing the tooth like smoke, a white elastic thread that looked like dental floss, and for a moment she imagined herself a magician pulling an endless silk from her mouth. She felt her gorge rise and closed her eyes, opened her mouth enormously wide, letting the tooth drop to the floor, gripped the toilet's sides with both hands, and burped.

Opening her eyes Bethany saw Jesus of Nazareth standing before her in a white undershirt, swimming trunks and flip-flops.

Bethany was ecstatic but flustered. 'I didn't

ask God to send you or even rub a lamp.'

'A tooth, I see, yes.' Jesus motioned to the sink with his goatee'd chin while yanking the last strand of elastic – that keeping his trunks up – from her mouth. 'Teeth. The last one, huh?'

Bethany nodded. 'Yes, Jesus. Do you want a grilled cheese?'

'What you said – no, no grilled cheese just yet, though I might take you up on that later! – but what you said is true, Bethany. If your teeth are rotting then so are mine. I.e. look at that bicuspid.' He pointed to one on the sink. 'That cavity has been plaguing us for weeks. I'm almost out of Vicodin.'

Bethany laughed. 'So cast that cavity from the temple, Jesus!'

'The temple of our teeth?'

'Yes, Jesus.'

'Mm, all right, a stretch but, here, just, right-'

Jesus and Bethany scrubbed and scraped and dug at her teeth until they were free of cavities, using a quick drying cement Jesus found in her dad's workshop for the fillings.

When they had finished Bethany hugged Jesus. She hugged him with a big stretch of her skinny arms, wrapping them around Jesus' sunburned torso. 'Thanks for helping me, Jesus.'

'Sure, Bethany.' He chuckled. 'Where, oh cavity, is thy pang? Where, oh death, is thy- Ouch!'

'Sorry, Jesus.' Bethany sheepishly withdrew the offending, pinching hand as he rubbed his left buttock.

He winced. 'That *really* hurt.'

'Sorry, Jesus.'

'And now-'

Jesus helped Bethany put all but one of her teeth back in place.

'You go with this one, huh, Jesus?' She held aloft the hindmost unmoored molar.

He nodded, making strange motions with his hands, and was gone in the instant Bethany closed her eyes and sharply inhaled. A black renegade thread from Jesus' trunks hung for a moment from her lip like an errant spaghetti noodle before it was drawn firmly but delicately into her mouth, Bethany blinking and burping again.

She felt her stomach with her palm, a troubled look in her squinted eyebrows. 'Well, if my stomach is rumbling, then so is Jesus Christ's!' She never could have guessed what would summon him next.

Taking Short
or I Love You, Chelsea Manning
A Telepathic Chat Between Chelsea Manning and Jonah Jeffries
2011-05-01, 12:14EST

If you really want to hear about it, you'll probably want to know about how I used to stand in front of the mirror each morning, brushing my hair, inspecting for pimples, looking myself in the eye, thinking, 'My life is worthwhile, even if the NSA hates me.' Or thinking, 'I can't be fat when they come to strip me naked and torture me. I'll be so humiliated with all this excess weight.' But you can't ever start telling anyone anything, or you'll start to miss people all the time.

Yeah, well, I guess you're right, Chelsea. But you can think whatever you like. Think it right at me. Nothing too startling. Nothing shocking. Nothing that will make me love you less.

I suppose there is no difference between being monitored and *believing* that you are being monitored. This is why the FBI tries to convince us that they have an agent behind every signpost and refrigerator in the land. I personally have always tried not to strain and not to make any sound during my daily voiding, just in case.

Just in case they are listening and/or watching at that time.

Right. And the thousands of snitches involved in Operation: Ghetto Listening Post serve as reminder that even my forty dollar handshakes were privy to their knowledge.

Forty dollars? Those ain't New York City prices!

But anyway, if you really want to hear about it, here in penal captivity I have made some friends. At least here in Ft. Leavenworth, my second correctional facility. The first, in Virginia, was not so pleasant. There, many of the guards hated me so much that they thought their mocking "renditions" of me were "extraordinary," and would imitate me at any given opportunity - usually just lip-syncing to Lady Gaga while looking at internet porn, but I knew what they were doing. And this on top of all of the required exercises which were part of my daily regimen: standing stationary for long periods of time (I think this improves the agility of particular leg muscles); one hour's worth of walking in the yard per day (although the ankle-chains inhibited my stride); and of course bedtime nudity – nothing prevents suicide like sleeping without skivvies!

At least they're not dressing you in a white shroud, Al-Sadr style.

On the contrary: That's my permanent outfit.

Then let me be the first to say, Peace be with you!
Sorry. Are the guards better or worse in Leavenworth? Or is that moot?

The guards here in Leavenworth are as amiable as the guards in Quantico, really. They're just following orders, after all, so I can't take it personally. I did, to be fair, betray the unwritten rule that you should never tell the truth about things everyone has already silently agreed to lie about. It is unforgiveable. Jones, my own personal guard here in Leavenworth, wryly told me that he receives one of two reactions when he brags about his "infamous" prisoner ("Who ain't even famous, much less *in*famous" he says). The first: Who the fuck is Chelsea Manning? The second: He did *what*? That fucker should be in Guantanamo.

Of course Jones is quick to educate others on the recent Supreme Court ruling that Guantanamo *is* subject to US law, even though it's not technically part of the United States. But that's the price of being everywhere – you can't pretend you aren't in places that you are!

Except for in Persia!

"Yes, but, Jones," I replied, "now they just send the prisoners to Bagram, which is out of the bounds of US law."

"Ain't the US acting in Bagram?"

"Yes, sir."

"So the Court is gonna have to declare that even Bagram is subject to US law?"

"Well yeah, but then the administration'll just declare some *other* black site, er prison is not subject to US law. Maybe we should just change the law."

"And make torture *legal*?" Jones was aghast as he slid my cell door closed.

"Why not? Our law book should state who we are – not who some of us would like to be. If we're into torture, let's just put it into the books. Put it into the constitution. Then we can at least know who we are – and if we don't like it, change it."

A real fart smeller, as they say.

Jones was n- Huh?

Fart smeller. Smart fella. You know.

Jones was not agreeable to this way of thinking. As a former service member himself, he says he did not swear to serve and protect a tortured constitution.

What about an extraordinarily renditioned one?

And me? I feel pretty well caught in the middle of the various tortures subjected by USAers to other USAers and non-USAers, alike. Sure, there are at any given moment tens-of-thousands of US prisoners serving time in Administrative Maximum Facilities, which means isolation and dehumanization. But why get so up in arms about dehumanization? The whole world is dehuman; why should we be different?

Because we are human, Chelsea. Do you need a nap?

Here I disagree with my Muslim friends, who largely see the unending War On Terror as the dehumanization of a *particular community*. This is true, of course, just ask Jose Padilla or Imam Luqman Ameen Abdullah – the latter unarmed and shot 21 times in his mosque, after which a wounded police dog was airlifted to a hospital while the Imam lay bleeding and handcuffed on the floor, eventually expiring to Allah.

Further, once actions that are not terroristic are re-defined as terroristic, I maintain that the yield of possible terrorists would be the same whether in a Muslim community in Queens or a quilting circle in Oregon.

Nevertheless, it is not only the Muslims who are being dehumanized. Doesn't it dehumanize all of us to participate in dehumanizing activities against others? I'm not trying to be glib here, I swear! The difference, really, is that the Muslims don't get to have any fun being dehumanized; whereas the rest of us can mostly escape with our throats uncut and our lives not behind bars – although we leave behind our dignity, and liberty, and privacy. But pish-posh on all that sentimentalism! As Zeke, one of the Guantanamo attorneys, instructed me years ago: There is no justice, there is just a game that you play.

And no, I don't need a nap.

You're a freedom fighter.

It is often said that one man's Freedom Fighter is another man's Terrorist. It is also true that one man's Whistleblower is another man's Aider Of The Enemy. To allow the general population to know what the government is doing in the general population's name – is this Whistleblowing or Aiding The Enemy? This largely depends on what is revealed. To the current Hawaiian incumbent, there is not a whistle in the country that can be blown – unless for a blissful public relations photograph with the dog! Just ask Thomas Drake, or Shamai Kedem Leibowitz. Or wait, you've never heard of them so never mind.

Meanwhile, those of us trying to reveal the nature of the world and the actions that are happening in the world are chastised by The Paper for "nearly delusional grandeur unmatched by an awareness that the digital secrets revealed can have a price in flesh and blood." The price in flesh and blood for *not* revealing those secrets? That is a question better unasked. After all, The Paper admits it can be "overly credulous" sometimes, specifically about "some of the prewar reporting about Iraq's supposed weapons of mass destruction." Oh, the cost in flesh and blood of being overly credulous!

Well, if you're not credulous enough you could have a real bloodbath on your hands. Don't be delusional.

It seems The Paper cannot talk enough about our delusions. When writing about my friends, The Paper claims that "friends say they wonder whether his desperation for acceptance – or delusions of grandeur – may have led him to disclose the largest trove of government secrets since the Pentagon Papers." That this was done for political or moral reasons is not to be considered – only personal shortcomings could have led a weenie of a USAer into such truth-telling!

I don't think they called you a weenie.

There can be nothing more hilarious (aside from taking short, of course) than Admiral Mullen's concern that I "might already have on my hands the blood of some young soldier or that of an Afghan family." This from the gentleman in charge of just thousands of sorties over Afghanistan? The terrorizing and humiliating night raids? And an astounding number of soldier rapes by other soldiers? And soldier suicides?

Who was it that noted that a few deaths are a tragedy, while millions of deaths are a blurb?

Benny Hill?

I mean, Christ All Mighty, I was just telling everyone- No! Not Benny Hill, for Christ's sake, Jonah!

All right, all right. You were just telling everyone... ?

Right, I was just telling everyone the awful shit that I'd found out. *Hey!,* I tried to yell to everyone I'd ever known or didn't know but loved because they were a part of the world, too, *Hey! Hey, Everyone! We got sold out! Hey! Hey! They lied to us and we believed it! Hey! Hey, they're lying to us and killing us and brutalizing us! Hey! I found this fucked up shit that we do every day! Hey! Look! Over here!*

We're busy, Chelsea. Knock that shit off. It's not real. Or there's nothing we can do about it. Or nothing should *be done about it. Or whatever. Don't ruin it for the rest of us.*

Can you imagine a wedding in the US – I mean a *big* wedding, outside, with all sorts of tables and cakes and chairs and water fountains and fancy clothing – in the middle of a sunshiny day somewhere in freedom's land: and suddenly an

Afghan drone from a nearby Afghan military base (maybe located in Winnipeg or something) flies over and bombs the whole party? Can you imagine? If you read the documents I found and shared with everyone, you could. The Paper cannot imagine it, and they say and report such laughable and striking things, without laughing or striking, like:

There was "every indication this was a group of terrorists, not a charity carwash in the hinterlands." (Every indication! And how every *evidence*?)

Or, "This was a group of terrorists. We're not talking about a bunch of guys who were playing pinochle at the local Kiwanis club." (I think over there it might be *Chor Voli* at the Charahi Qambar refugee camp.)

Or, "These people weren't gathering for a bake sale. They were terrorists." I suppose then, that they'd better start serving baked goods at the Arms Distributor Fair, or watch out, the arm of justice will swoop down in an unmanned drone and murder citizens without a warrant, without a charge, without a single shred of evidence.

I love my country – at least the people *in it* – and would never want to dishonor it, or even give cause for alarm that dishonor might exist within it, and that is why I can so clearly and with a mind as sound as sardines state that I hoped they would just string me up like John Brown.

Is there a high horse in this cell of yours that you keep riding in on?

Oh fuck you, Jonah. I'm rotting in this fucking cell for one of the most selfless acts in the history of human-fucking-kind. If I wanna get up on a horse and fuck it, I'm gonna.

. . .

What was that? You couldn't hear me over the hum of your microwave dinner and the din from the internet channel you're watching which is being dominated by the television show you're gaping in front of in your not-manned-by-armed-guards apartment?

All right, all right. You're not on a high horse and I was being short-sighted and hard on you and easy on me.

There is one gentleman they've been keeping at Guantanamo who has been described as more like a piece of furniture than a person. He has been tortured and lied to and bamboozled so many times that he cannot be convinced that his own lawyers aren't really government agents trying to gather information from him to be used against him.
And what would a Gitmo inmate have to tell? That they were victims of Radiofrequency Identification [RFID] chips, which young impoverished Afghans were paid by USAers to distribute anywhere al-Qaeda or Taliban were suspected to be? A bundle of dollars (or afghanis) for every time one of these chips is tossed somewhere? Sure, throw 'em around like confetti at a wedding party. In Dih Bala. On July 6, 2008. Here comes the bride. Burnt to a crisp.

That doesn't rhyme.

. . .

I can't believe you did something so brave and righteous and you're stuck in that rotting fucking cell. I love you, Chelsea Manning.

As the Dylan song goes: They cursed Jesus, too.

Yeah, but you're not him.

No?

. . .

After two decades of school in which we learn that there is some sort of society of *people* out there who care about you and me – and whom we care about . . . that there is a *we*, an *us* – eventually you learn that there's just you. There's no one to fall back on; there's no society to offer succor or support – only chastisements and punishments for following principles instead of ad hoc altruisms. Only admonishment for not bowing your head and doing what everyone else does. Do the righteous thing? Start shittin bricks.

Did you ever take short, Chelsea? I did, once.

. . .

Out for dinner. Chili. Long lavatory line. Figured I'd make it back to the house. Extended car trip home. Traffic. Then a bump on the road during an urgent fart. Kabloom.

The thing is, is that sometimes taking short is agonizing – and sometimes it is hilarious.

Only sometimes?

On the other hand Adnan Farhan Abd Al Latif, a pen-pal from down Guantanamo way, recently regaled me with tales of agony. Not only does he literally have to shit in a bucket as part of his daily ablutions, but he tells me that the forced sodomy also (on a good day) ends with the sensation of a massive voiding of the bowels. Of course, agonizing as this must have been, he at least could describe it to me, so it was not as bad as the "unspeakable tortures" which he, by definition, did not speak about.

It must be that our rulers and their operators think many of these acts are unspeakable, as well. For one, they rarely speak of them even though thousands are routinely tortured the whole world over with direct and indirect support from us. But when they want to speak of secret prisons, they call them "black sites." And when they want to describe kidnapping someone and sending them to a secret prison to be tortured, they call it "extraordinary rendition." And torture is "coercive / enhanced interrogation." And burglary? That's a "black bag job." And purposefully creating the false appearance that someone is a government operative? That's a "bad jacket." And killing someone illegally? That's "extralegal," don't you know!

Oh, we use all kinds of techniques to gather information; or just for something to do when we realize that information is not available from the source we have extraordinarily renditioned. This is called having access to The Full Toolbox. And what tools are used! Can't you just see it, dear Jonah, a tall and strong and free (and hopefully white!) United States citizen in full soldier's regalia proudly performing a mock execution! Or magnificently maneuvering a prisoner into a stress position; or heroically inducing hypothermia . Or electric shocks (which combine nicely with the sexual humiliation). Or the exquisite (and no doubt eloquent) death threats against prisoners and their families. Can't you just see the shining face of a brave USA soldier telling a shaking sweating bleeding hysterical prisoner that his family is in the next cell over receiving the same kind of house treatment? Oh, the delicious pride of being American, from sea to livid sea!

I really think you need a nap.

I need a dirt nap. And I'm not being dramatic. This world wants me out; and that is fine with me. I reciprocate the feeling.

This world wants you dirt-napping, fine. But not me, Chelsea. Not my friends; not my siblings. Not me, Chelsea. I love you, Chelsea Manning.

Do you love the 171 men rotting in Guantanamo? More than half of whom have been cleared of any wrongdoing for years, but they have no right to challenge their detention and have no chance of being released from their administrative hell?

Yes, yes, I love them, too, Chelsea. Them, too.

They arrested 1,200 men for pretextual immigration violations and shipped them to Gitmo. One gentleman was arrested because translating an Arabic newspaper into English was deemed support for al-Qaeda. Can you believe that shit, Jonah? He translated like the Afghan version of the *Village Voice* for the local library, and that's terrorism.

What would happen if he translated "Bong Hits for Jesus"?

Straight to Bagram with the motherfucker. Make him bark like a dog and maybe you'll get some useful intel out of him. Like how to make delicious hummus.

. . .

These are guys in Gitmo that they found any old place and rounded up. One 15 year-old kid who was defending his family's home from invading US soldiers – and he's a terrorist. They torture and question these poor bastards for years and years - and still mark on their forms "areas of potential exploitation" – as though there's anything left to humiliate and exploit after years of torture and abuse. You know they write down every thing each prisoner says about other prisoners? As though some kidnapped tortured asshole from one part of the Muslim world would necessarily know some other kidnapped tortured asshole from some other part of the Muslim world. And these are guys – according to the Director of National Intelligence – who "re-offend" only 15% of the time.

Isn't recidivism in the US justice system like 50%?

But it's their job to make sure there are valid reasons to keep the prisoners imprisoned, so they can keep interrogating them and inviting their intelligence officer friends from the whole wide world over to stop on by and shock a genital or smash someone's head into the wall!

Maybe spray around some sus scrofa.

Ha!
You know, Jonah, I used to like and think about Martin Luther King's interpretation of the Rip Van Winkle story: that Van Winkle had slept through a revolution. I feel like I've been tortured through a revolution – but it's only a personal revolution. Freedom's land remains un-revoluted.

But revolting!

You know, Jonah, out in the desert we once saw five Iraqi children save a pigeon at a stone well, before we blew it all up. It was the most beautiful image I had ever seen, just before my heart broke (which means that the heart has lost a magic that cannot be reimagined). Five children saved the desert pigeon, dust hanging in diamond glitters above the bird's splayed and broken but majestic wings, the stones of the well from the time of Mohammed or Abraham or whatever.

Then you blew up the well?

Those were the orders. We scattered the children with shouts and gunfire, blew up the well because we didn't know what was in it – water? – and the pigeon was collateral damage. Better than the five kids, I figured at the time, even though my heart was still breaking.

I don't understand why they want you, and not The Paper.

Publishing secrets is not really a crime. That's why they are chasing me and Julian – because we leaked the documents. That's easier to prosecute than publishing. Plus it's easier to go after me and WikiLeaks than The Paper. And there's no shortage of respected people who hate leaks. The head of the project on government secrecy at the Federation of American Scientists regards WikiLeaks as "among the enemies of open society because it does not respect the rule of law nor does it honor the rights of individuals." I mean, their fucking *stated mission* is to "challenge excessive government secrecy and to promote public oversight," and they are *opposed* to WikiLeaks.

That's some memory you have, Chelsea.

I've had nothing to do for years but remember.

Does the Federation of American Scientists honor the rights of individuals?

Ask the US Public Health Service. Or anyone from Tuskegee.

I guess "open society" means one where our rulers act in our name without us having any even general idea of what those actions are?

Terrorist! Communist! Anarchist! Wobbly! Okay okay, I had to get those out of the way.

Aside from Terrorist, I would be flattered by any of those. I wish we could apply the word to those who deserve it most – the State Department; and the assholes that fly the drones.

Which even according to the Navy and the UK Ministry of Defense will be acting in ways uncontrollable by humans in the coming years.

Meaning that robots will take over?

Not exactly. Meaning that robots will be designed and programmed to act faster than a human being can ascertain, interpret and, if needed, interfere with.

You think there'll be a whistleblowing robot?

Only if it's the tea-kettle, brother.

Did you have a favorite leaked document?

No.
Actually, my favorite one is not current; it's from COINTELPRO. I quote: "The Bureau is requested to prepare and furnish to Detroit in liquid

form a solution capable of duplicating a scent of the most foul smelling feces available. In this case, it might be appropriate to duplicate the feces of the species *sus scrofa*. A quart supply, along with a dispenser capable of squirting a narrow stream for a distance of approximately three feet would satisfy the needs of the proposed technique."

I love that one. Poor Detroit.

I almost feel bad for the G-men on that one. Almost. I always wondered what banal joke they played on who, and in what space. I bet it smells worse than Fallujah.

Do they have a sewage problem there?

Do they ever, brother. Particularly after we bombed all three wastewater treatment plants.

Shit.

Totally. You know 80% of the population of Fallujah are refugees? I mean, the ones still on the surface of the planet. One of my buddies said his company commander ordered them to, "Shoot everything that moves and everything that doesn't move."

Sounds like that Kissinger line about telling the Air Force in Cambodia: "Anything that flies on anything that moves."

Quite a barbecue in Fallujah, to be sure. We also took out their two bridges, both train stations, both electricity stations. Plus the entire communication and sanitation systems. Just stone-age bombing with snipers picking off any body that dared to be alive after the city was flattened. 36,000 houses, 9,000 shops, 65 mosques, 60 schools, libraries, government offices. We had to destroy it to destroy it, you know? More is more. Then less is less.

Where did you get those statistics? Did you leak those too? Ha!

No. Har har.
If you're in the US you can obtain the information by special ordering a very expensive book from an Australian publisher. No, really, that's how easy it is to obtain information about our own actions!
In some neighborhoods, like al-Shutra, US forces were making films about the conquering of Fallujah, and needed footage of like destroying a house or something, but they already had control of the place. So we just blew up "abandoned" houses for the film as though it were a real combat situation. And then paid $4,000 per house.

How much is a house worth in Fallujah? Is that generous?

About as generous as the military usually is. Most houses were worth about $50,000 in that neighborhood. And that's just the house – no furniture or accoutrements or anything.
We even bombed the building where the hospital's back-up supplies were stored. Twice.

Maybe they didn't know what it was.

Of course we knew what it was. They told us what it was and where it was so that we wouldn't bomb it.

But why a hospital?

According to *The Economist*, it was because during the First Gulf War hospitals reported that hundreds of civilians had been killed, quite an inconvenient PR snafu to explain. Or explain away.

One Army buddy told me that he spent the majority of his time in Iraq crossing and recrossing the Jurf Kas Sukr Bridge, shitting his pants. He said it with a straight face and I didn't dare laugh.

You know, my brother, GK, one time took short right after church. I was sitting in the dining room of our house, the only one home since everyone was still getting out of the Sunday morning service. And I heard the backdoor fly open, and GK in a blur shot through the kitchen and then, instantly, stopped in the doorway, two steps from the bathroom.

He stopped, one leg bent and knee pointing to the welcoming but too distant bathroom door.

He stopped, his right arm flung up as though pointing to the now no longer urgently needed bathroom door, his left arm held out in front of him as though he were an athlete on the football field breaking tackles.

He stopped, and sighed, an awful but hilarious grimace of heartbreak on his face – and a slight grin of begrudging humor – nothing urgent anymore in his expression, but only resignation.

. . .

Do you regret it? Now that you've been a plaything of the justice system for years on end?

I wouldn't mind going to prison for the rest of my life, or being executed so much, if it wasn't for the possibility of having pictures of me plastered all over the world press.
When they put me under suicide watch and checked me every five minutes, just for funsies, you know, that wasn't my best time.

Yeah, I heard they let you sleep uninterrupted from 10pm to 5am, though.

Sure. Unless they needed to make sure I was alive, you know, since I was on suicide watch and all.

How often did they need to make sure you were alive?

Every five minutes.

Plus they forced you to sleep naked, right?

. . .

Chelsea, this is just a telepathic talk. Just you and me, brother. And I'm hardly even real.

Me too, brother.

I read that the Pentagon said you weren't in solitary confinement because they let you shout to other prisoners in your cellblock.

We used White Phosphorous in Fallujah, too. Wily Pete, we called it. From Camp American University to Fallujah.

Camp America, you mean the official name of Gitmo?

Yeah, that too, Jonah.

Did I just hear your mind sigh?

If you can read my mind, Jonah, then you know that Camp America is Gitmo, and Camp American University is where we started manufacturing chemical weapons, right around the time Winston Churchill was first using mustard gas on Iraqis. Or Kurds. Ottomans?

God, I can hear The Paper calling you a disillusioned, disgruntled single Army private discontent with the military and American foreign policy. And bla bla bla. (You can't see but I'm making copious jerk-off motions.)

Thanks for letting me know.
You can see that being disillusioned is bad, according to The Paper. Instead we should be illusioned, I guess. We should be overly credulous. I should've pledged allegiance to one nation under God and done my Scriptural homework!

You didn't?

No, I always refused that stuff.

I didn't. I pledged to the flag every week – the Christian flag, too. And memorized a Bible verse every week, to boot. My friend Kayeeth used to cheat on those with aplomb.

What's the Christian flag pledge?

I pledge allegiance to the Christian flag, and to the savior for whose kingdom it stands. One savior, crucified, risen and coming again with life and liberty for all who believe.

Yuck. Those pledges. . . How can you trust someone who takes such a pledge, from youth onward, without question? The Christians are always harping on their youth not to give their sexuality away without searching to know that pure is pure and true is true. But the nation? Pledge away, no investigation needed.

Well, come on, Chelsea, it's the USA, not some hideous place like Egypt.

You ever read *The Blackboard*?

N-

Of course you didn't. It was a phony "underground" newspaper. It featured stories about community leaders and activists, mostly slanderous, about sexual matters usually, the prudes. The FBI made and distributed it, although of course pretending that it *wasn't* the FBI.
You ever hear of Karen Sullivan?

N-

Of course you didn't. It was a fake name. She worked with anti-war groups in Minneapolis, the Twin Cities Anti-War Committee: chairing committees, bookkeeping, communications, on and on. For two and a half years. Then she disappeared overnight, just before the September morning in 2010 when the FBI raided the homes of anti-war activists nationwide, including Minneapolis.

You ever hear of the Maryland State Police spying on peace and anti-death penalty activists?

N-

Of course you didn't.

They classified 53 nonviolent activists as terrorists in state and federal databases for tracking terrorists. Activists protesting Lockheed Martin were monitored. By the Maryland State Police.

You ever hear of the Committee for the Expansion of Socialist Thought in America?

N-

Of course you haven't. It was a fictional organization set up by the FBI in 1965 to provoke arguments and in-fighting amongst the Communist Party.

Did you ever hear of Lori Paton?

N-

Of course you haven't. 15 year old kid who wrote a letter to the Socialist Party asking for information, and was investigated by FBI agents for the infraction.

That would make for quite a Civics class presentation. Good morning class, here are the political police- er, the FBI!

Do you know how many college and University campuses the CIA is on?

You mean, like, to scope out chicks and Muslims?

Sorta. Jerk-off. A CIA spokesperson once bragged that "the CIA has enough professors under Agency contract to staff a large university."

They never recruited me!

Okay, so they don't do *everything* wrong. Hurrah.

I really think you need a nap.

Did you know that the FBI follows around college students and activists, digging through their trash? Following them to bars, parks, libraries, staking out residences, videotaping.

Mama's gonna keep baby healthy and clean!

Thank you for the Pink Floyd reference. But there's nothing comfortable about how numb all this shit makes me.
You ever hear of Thomas Curran?

N-

Of course you haven't. A stooge for the FBI who took the stand to testify against people the FBI didn't very much like, each time pretending to be some other professional. One time he was a biologist, then a zoologist, then a psychologist. Whatever the occasion needed for justice to be served.

You ever heard of the Security Index? Or the Rabble Rouser Index? Or the Agitator Index?

Um-

Have you?

No.

. . .

Those sound fake.

They're not. They're real. And on the public record. But you don't know about them. Your name could be on there, but you don't know about it. They take away your freedom and you don't even care to know that they have done so. In your own blessed New York City the NYPD has a "professional agitators" list.

I know that power does awful things to maintain and increase its own power. But you just seem to be talking paranoid shit.

When several men in Gitmo killed themselves - for obvious reasons - US Deputy Assistant Secretary of State for Public Diplomacy Colleen Graffy literally said: "Taking their own lives was not necessary, but it certainly was a good PR move." *She literally believes that their suicides were part of a PR campaign to make torturing people look bad.*

Okay, that does sound more than innocuous.

At Guantanamo, they literally have dog cages in vans that they transport prisoners in. Dog cages. And suicide is some mystery.
I already mentioned Operation Ghetto Listening Post, also known as the Ghetto Informant Program. At least 3,248 snitches in the "ghettos" of the United States. We divide and conquer well.
You ever heard of Tommy the Traveler?

N-

Of course you haven't.
Thomas Tongyai went from campus to campus, all over upstate New York, trying to lure activist students, or just plain crazies, into violent actions. When Tommy was the only one committing the violent actions, they made him into a cop.
You ever hear of Grupo pro-USO VOTO del MPR?

What the fuck are you-

Of course you haven't.
It was a phony political group in Puerto Rico, advocating for PR to stay under US rule, while the whole country opposed it. Since it was the FBI and not really Puerto Ricans, they killed PRs; shot PRs; blew up PR offices; threatened people. *¡Si se puede!*

Didn't you ever worry that someone would be hurt from the leaked files?

Sure, I did. I also worried that someone would be hurt from the *not*-leaked files. Also, Defense Secretary Gates already admitted that no one was put in jeopardy from the leaks.

Yeah, but Admiral Mullen said that you have the blood of some young soldier or an Afghan family on your hands.

That's like King George pretending to worry about the lives of colonists. The day Admiral Mullen gives a damn about some young soldier or an Afghan family I will personally free all the guys in Gitmo with the help of a risen and glorified Jesus H Christ, high on caffeine and ganja, lighting smokes with disciplinary citations for inappropriate use of bodily fluids.

Great day in the mornin!

The Paper may anticipate with dread that day we learn that someone identified in the leaked documents has been killed (because of the leaked documents, presumably), but The Paper does not dread or even regret the support given for a hideous war in which not "someone" but millions of "someones" have been killed, beaten, raped, tortured, refugeed, diseased and bulldozed into oblivion.

You must be going batshit crazy in those close quarters, brother.

One time, in Leavenworth, I thought it'd be funny if I shat into a bag, lit it on fire, and tossed it outside the cell into the passageway for a guard to stomp out with his big-ass boots. But I didn't have a bag or a shirt or anything at all to toss a shit into – let alone to light it.

Or any shit. Am I right? Am I right?

. . .

You know, 'cause the food is bad?

You know, Jose Padilla said that when he was beaten by the guards and interrogators, they would look at him like a lover in the middle of coitus, as though they were thinking something pleasant like, "I will get here with you again and again." This was before he was "like a piece of furniture," as they said.

You mean Jorge Posada?

No.
In the end, he wasn't even sure if his own lawyers were his real lawyers or if they were government interrogators pretending to be his lawyers. We already went over this.

Shit. Reminds me of I heard that in the last days Hitler was so paranoid that he suspected his suicide cyanide pills were phony. In other words, he was concerned that someone was out to keep him alive*! Crazy fucker.*

But he got his just dues at the Supreme Court.

Hitler?

No, the other guy.

Jorge Posada?

No, asshole, you know, the one we're talking about – Jose Padilla. Poor bastard.

What are Supreme Court just dues?

The court heard his case and ruled on the injustice of it all.

No. They threw out the case as no longer relevant, since after three years held in detention without charge and almost two years without a lawyer, he was finally going to be charged. It's a principled Court.

. . .

You think I'm a paranoid.

But I don't think of that as a negative thing. I get paranoid whenever I think that the frames on the wall are didactically level, as though someone has been futzing with them to make them appear un-futzed with.

I don't need paranoia. *I'm Chelsea Manning.* The officer who reads my mail before I do is so caustic he has started adding lipstick-kisses to my envelopes – whether from my mom or *The Blackboard*. He has also begun facetiously stamping the letters with "Inspected by yo' Inspector."

Classy.

If I so much as scratch my balls I have to hear jokes like "Yo, Manning, is this a race towards blindness of loneliness?" Or if I sit on the shitter for a half-second they'll call out, "Can we get a courtesy flush up in here, please?"
I usually just call out, "There's no Vickie Weaver's here!" It gets a laugh; from me, at least.
Of course there was the time that I sat down and found plastic wrap stretched across the mouth of the open toilet bowl. Another joke from the guards. That totally modern sound of liquid on polyvinyl chloride, slipping with friction.

Liquid?

Well, wouldn't you be shitting yourself into such a state if you were me, Jonah?

I would be the liquid.

That night they also short-sheeted my bed. The bastards.

They let you have sheets?

No, I was joking.
But did you know that in Palestine the IDF breaks into people's-

The what?

The IDF: Israeli Defense Forces. They break into people's apartment buildings in the middle of the night, photograph children over 10 years old, so that they can later identify which child threw a stone at a riot cop. Or IDFer.

Fucking Christ, do you ever have any good news, Chelsea?

All my news is good news, brother. You just don't know how to receive it.

. . .

Sometimes at Leavenworth I felt the urge to throw out all of my toothbrushes, fearing they'd been shoved into nefarious guard cavities. But then I remembered they didn't let me have a toothbrush, so no worries.

Your teeth must be mossy. And hurt.

It's a strange phenomenon to say, "Ow, that hurts" – as one might say to a friend or sibling that you were horsing around with – and to realize that the pain is the point of what is being done to you; not just an unintended product of something that is good for you like an inoculation. "You are hurting me" is no longer the last defense against further hurt, but confirmation of success.

I'm sorry.

Sometimes I remember my love. I remember his smile one late night when a bunch of friends were camping at a state park. A blackness around us mildly illuminated by a tenacious bug lamp. Far beyond the thick oak trunks and hovering budding foliage were the campground's foul kiddy pond and the other residents' sleeping mobile homes. In the light from the bug lamp, I smiled at him. He was giddily drunken and smiling, his wide brown pupils below and beside and above the scattering rivers of his dark hair, falling one way another. As it happened I remembered to remember it, to save it for later. And to let myself be afraid of something greater than I – not just something more powerful. Above us, blooms and blooms enveloping.

Then he farted and accidentally shit his pants.

Aww, fucker, Chelsea! That was a romantic tale!

Leavenworth is complete paradise after the initial holding cell in Quantico. At Leavenworth I don't just get a room with a toilet, but drinking water to boot, taken directly from the toilet bowl with cupped hands.

Sometimes I feel like Gideon in here, Jonah. Because much like the Old Testament warrior I too hunch down and scoop water with my hands; I don't get down on my knees and drink directly like some barbarian!

Do you need to see a doctor?

Oh no, the medical staff here is out of this world! I've never been so well taken care of. You should see how quickly Dr. Brehm can heal a massive scalded burn. Or how Dr. Behnke can set a broken bone faster than you could holler "Hey that hurts like a motherfucker!" And the dental extractions-

Holy Christ, Chelsea.

And sometimes, when they want me to stay awake for extended periods of time, they play music and other noises at very loud volume, to help me not sleep. Stuff like George Formby's "Imagine Me in the Maginot Line" or Freddie "Boom Boom" Cannon. Finger-snapping stuff, to be sure.

Huey Piano Smith & the Clowns?

Most definitely!
Sometimes we practice creative relaxation positions, which I test to make sure the positions are such that there is no relaxing.

What would you do with freedom?

I don't know. It's. . . it's so remote a possibility. It's like asking me what I would do with a billion dollars. Or toilet paper.
I remember one of the Gitmo guys telling me about his arrest. He said they came to his home, and he tried to offer them beverages or a snack, but the sock one of them had taken (with delicacy!) from his newly broken foot and ankle and placed into his mouth to soak up the blood from the wrecked face and mouth they had bestowed on him – the sock just wouldn't allow for speech! He did, eventually, work the sock out with his tongue before vomiting broken teeth and blood all over himself in an effusive effort to offer snacks and beverages to the USA soldiers.

This is some account.

I got nothing to do all day but bullshit with other poor motherfuckers, Jonah. What's your excuse?

. . .

So anyway, loose as saloon doors and the people who part them (I knew somone who used to say that), his two front teeth flipped up and almost out when he managed to work the sock out of his mouth. He said he tried to make a joke, after vomiting on himself and shitting his pants, something like "Which one of you guys is picking up the dry cleaning tab?" but it just sounded like, "Ffffsssssppppttttt."

You're my fucking hero. I don't mean it ironically.

I'm just an Army Intelligence Analyst from the Second Brigade of the 10th Mountain Division from Contingency Operating Station Hammer, east of Babylon. Er, Baghdad.

You're the kind of outlaw it really takes guts to be.

As Muqtada al-Sadr would say, If I am an outlaw according to the American legal code, then I take pride in it.

Your manuscript cannot be burnt, brother.

Hey Jonah, I've got to go. Others need my attention.

Julian?

No. Others. Nameless. Faceless. But with agency, anyway. Like all of us. The agency of any individual is so vast the state spends countless dollars trying to suppress each one of us. It's inspiring, really.

Inspiring as a hanging.

A hanging interrupted.

You know, I heard when you hang you-

Take short? Totally. The shitstorm for power from my lynching will never be cleaned up. And will overshadow and outshine any office-holder or ass-kisser they can muster. Kabloom.

Bedford & First

Leora wanted to give me twenty dollars for the wine and cheese I had brought to the party. Her husband Derik agreed with me, though to little effect.

'Leora, I not only don't *need* the twenty dollars – or at least I can *afford* to part with it – but I *want* to contribute the wine and cheese to the party, as we prearranged.' We had done so only hours before, by phone.

Derik belched, his feet on the coffee table, jeans unbuttoned, shirtless, soft hand on a swollen belly. I was the last party-goer to exit. 'Yeah, babe. Aahp.' 'Aahp' was the sound he made when burping during discourse. 'It was prearranged. Gimme the twenty.'

I swatted Leora's hand away from my back pants pocket while buttoning my sweater. She giggled in a confident manner which meant giving me the twenty dollars was too pleasurable for her to contemplate keeping it.

She attempted to look directly and seriously into my eyes, as though to say it wasn't all modesty and ha-ha's. I was taking the twenty dollars whether I liked it or not. 'You don't even drink wine,' she said, accusingly.

'He eats cheese! Aahp. Gimme the twenty!'

'Listen to your husband. Keep it. I eat cheese!'

'He's a cheese eater, baby! Don't ever tell him a secret!'

'Your husband: a sage. And lo,' I pointed towards Derik, my arm extending across the sidebar that quartered the kitchen, 'his wine doth run low.' She promptly filled his glass while I crept the short hallway of the apartment towards the door, called

'Goodnight!' and exited down the stairs and into Brooklyn.

....

I have only guesses as to how Derik's general apathy towards the twenty dollars was converted to a longing to give it away – so much so that he stood from the couch, if not buttoned he at least *wore* his pants, and stepped out onto the fire-escape, two floors up. The black and rust-red stairs of the fire-escape zigzagged the five story building to the roof, one of the highest in the developing neighborhood.

But it was converted, Derik's general apathy, by Leora's giddy hook and prurient crook, I could be certain.

The heavy red door to the street slammed behind me, the frame cringing. I heard it a second time and could not turn around to see Leora before hearing from above, 'Babe, he's on the sidewalk right in front of you, babe.'

I looked up through the slats of the fire escape to see Derik's sockless white feet and scratchy-bearded face. 'You bastard!' I shook my fist.

Swatting Leora's two-handed go for my back pocket I walked quickly away, hoping my urban stride in sneakers would trump her's in turquoise heels. She laughed (tee-hee'd?) with a frightful genuineness. Street lights, and lights from the laundromat and the bodega, lit the warm night. I was twenty-seven and Leora was twenty-six. As I aged, a bachelor, I often lost sight of what was appropriate in male/female interactions, like if it were unseemly to encourage a twenty-six year old woman – lightly toasted – in high heels to chase me through Brooklyn. But she *did* have a look-out while I only had asthma.

'He's turning right, babe, down Grand. Run, baby, faster! Get him!' Derik jumped in place excitedly and then climbed to the roof – careful not to scratch his shirtless torso against the jagged rusty metal – where he was not omniscient but had a pretty good look at North Brooklyn.

'I'd be all broken ankles and chipped sidewalk teeth in those heels!' I called behind me, my head beginning to ache from shifting my eyes ahead and then behind, back and forth, furtively monitoring Leora's persistent tread.

She giggled and did not seem to increase her pace but did so. Marriage had made her invincible.

I ran across Grand as the bus approached the light, leaving her behind.

'He's across Grand, babe! He's running up Driggs, babe!' His voice became hysterical, cracking into high pitches; yet masculine from the back of the throat. 'Wait for the bus, babe! Wait! Okay, babe, go, he's running up Driggs, babe! Towards the park. Aahp!'

'The twenty is yours! It's yours!' I called behind me, eyes wide and wild. Frenzied. She giggled, covering her mouth with a gloved hand.

'Come here, Mr. Wine and Cheese. Twenty, twenty dollars, please.' It rang, as though sung, a cooing nightsong.

'He's going left on Fourth, babe! Left! Take a left on Metropolitan to Third and cut him off at Bedford! I bet he's going for the loop, babe, he's going for the loop!'

It wasn't the shrillness in Derik's yelps that brought people to the street and the fire escapes – or at least the open windows – to see the happening, but its persistence. Most everyone heard screaming a few times each day, but rarely with such sustained effrontery.

I intended to go left on Bedford where I would encounter two bus stops – and a bus?, oh, B61, if you've ever been a lady to begin with! – before crossing First to their block again, hoping to use the pedestrian traffic to impede Leora's progress.

'Run, babe! He's coming back around like I said! Just like I said, babe! Hurry to Bedford, baby! He's heading back this way!'

Not even the familiar squeal of bus brakes from some *other* block or neighborhood was heard as I hurried, dodging young men and ogling young women, jumping over fire hydrants and ducking under awnings.

'Babe, stop at the bagel shop and get me a coffee, will ya?'

'Hon, later!'

'Okay, okay, you're right, later, unless-' Derik called out to three employees who had gathered outside the entrance to the shop, the warm smell of bread blessing the street. 'Hey, can you guys... Do you guys deliver?'

One of the employees shook his head.

'Leora!' On the Avenue, because of the traffic I had hoped would be helpful, I was having to watch where I was headed – what came at me from the front – more than where I had been. 'Leora! Twenty dollars doesn't even cover a good bottle of wine! It's not like I brought some fancy *bourgeois* variety.'

'Oh, twenty isn't enough?' She smiled ferociously. 'Hon! Twenty's not enough! Throw down another! I'm coming around!'

I stood on the corner of First and Bedford watching Leora, open-mouthed and looking upward, watching a second twenty dollar bill flutter and fall the five stories. Light from street lamps and automobiles illuminated the bill in flickers and flashes in its descent. Leora laughed, eyes flitting from the bill to Derik, her skin lovingly lit by the neon from the bodega. She took steps one way and then back, trying to remain beneath the bill.

'Let's get a truce going here, Leora. My asthma wants out.'

'Never surrender, babe!' *What* agreement had they made?

'Leora, I'm gonna walk home, find my inhaler, abuse myself, and go to sleep. The next time there is a party or get together *you* can provide the wine and cheese and I'll purchase something else. Put those goddamn twenties away and quit walking towards me with that smirky, adorable grin!'

'Get him, babe! Get him!'

'Forty dollars coming at you, Mr. Wine and Cheese.'

'It's not mine to take! Stop! Don't place one foot gently in front of the other in a sultry saunter to my breathless crumpling body!'

'He's defenseless, babe! Look at him! He can hardly breathe! Get him, babe! Shove those twenties in his ass pockets! Sucks to your assmar, Jonah! Sucks to your assmar!'

'Leora! I'm gonna crawl home, suck down a tube of inhalant, read a book, toss one off, say a prayer and go to sleep, so don't bring that goddamn money any closer to my goddamned person.'

'Should of thought of that before buying all that cheese and wine, Mr. Wine and Cheese.'

'No! No!'

'Get him, babe! Yeah, that's it, shove those twenty's in his ass pockets, babe! Yeah! Fuck yeah, babe!'

A whoop of applause was heard around Bedford and First in the swelling night as Leora stabbed two twenty dollar bills into my pants' back pocket and I lay crumpled on the sidewalk, longing for a hit from the antiquated MDI inhaler.

'Your next Albuterol is on us, Mr. Forty Dollars.'

'Come on, babe! Come on inside now! He'll be fine. The bus is due in like twenty minutes! Remember what you promised!'

Eveline

She was frankly beautiful, Jonah thought. Like milk.
'I'll show you how the cow eats cabbage.'
Eveline was ambitious.
'Oh, sorry, is this all right?'
'Yes, it's fine, Jonah. Why do you do it and *then* ask?'
'...'
'Why do I do it and then ask? That's what you asked?'
'Mm hm.'
'I'm assuming . . . any time I manage to maneuver this into that, you know, it's because there is no problem. If there were a problem there's no way I'd get so far as to have the opportunity to-'
'Maneuver that into this?'
'Mm.'
'But you still ask.' Eveline was exact.
'For total clarity and awareness.'
'Your is the more beautiful way. As always.'
She quoted himself to himself – about her.
Jonah tried explaining to Eveline, who looked bemused, that any explanation from him was bound to be full of other explanations because he was a circle. He liked circles. There was no choice but circles. Evy sighed. She said, 'It's like the word "esoteric." It's self-fulfilling, you know? To even know what the words means. . .' She had confessed to him once that she could not tell the difference, on a recording, between a real violin and a synthesized violin. 'What does that mean?' she asked. 'What if you can't tell the difference?'
With great diligence, Jonah wrote something down.
'How can you be so intimate and so distant,

at once?'
' I was going to ask you the same thing, baby.'
He cleared his throat.
'But instead you answered saying. . .'
'...'
'Mm?' Persistent.
Jonah wondered from what delusion her confusion emanated. This was the woman who had told him that she never wanted to make love. Even with me, Evy?, he'd asked. Even with me you don't want this? Or *especially* with me?
'Especially,' she'd replied.
'Right.'
Some of Eveline's books and movies, piled on the bookcase flanking the bed, which was short and fat, the bookcase, and not at all perturbed by the heaving bed, jostled but did not fall. She liked all kinds of movies and stories that could not possibly take place under the laws of this world. Stories that she had experienced in childhood or which made her feel as though she had. Stories about adventures in warehouses or castles or undergrounds or witches dens – with all sorts of flights and fires and ghosts and moons. All stories were true, Evy thought, somewhere, in someone.
'The word esoteric,' she hearkened back, 'the self-fulfilling. Is that onomatopoeia?'
Jonah reminded her that he rarely got to spend time with anyone's vagina.
'I don't think,' she changed the subject, 'that someone who was really losing their mind would actually say, 'I am losing my mind.' They would just go ahead and lose it.'
'I think you are unnecessarily photogenic.'
'But I think I am losing my mind. From you. Not with you. From.'

'Like a virus.'

'Mm.'

Eveline was thinking, dimly, as in moments before sleep, about how they had gotten into each other's way the afternoon of their first meeting, in a hallway at school. She stepping one way to get out of his way and he stepping the same way to get out of hers, until he'd taken her shoulders in his hands and spun them in a half-circle, smiled and continued on. It had made her feel valuable, breakable. After that, she thought, I'd said that stupid thing about traffic, wanting to impress him. 'In theory that's how traffic works,' she remembered. I said that. He couldn't let it go. Wouldn't. Theories on traffic. Whose theories? I dunno. It was something to say. He's never forgotten. Probably thinking it now.

She mouthed the word 'traffic' at him, but his eyes were closed.

'Mm. . . hey, can you, yeah, just, your leg up, right, good, thanks.'

'Better?'

'Mm.'

'...'

'...'

One of dozens of notepads fell from the desk on the room's far side, onto the floor, disrupting momentarily with a loud snap the ambience created by the gentle and consistent buzz of the oscillating fan. Eveline referred to writing in the notebooks as 'realizing,' which Jonah had said was 'Fucking apt.' The pages were flipped and blown by the fan. Jonah's eyes peered for her handwriting, but the room was too dark.

'Do you think about me being with others?' Jonah was curious.

'Of course.'

'Does it make you jealous?'

'On occasion. If you're not around.'

'But when I'm right here.'

'I'm the one to be envied, in this context, at least. Does this non-jealousy bother you?' She was curious too.

'Ah,' he balked. 'I cannot conceive of somebody missing me; it's like I don't believe in it. My life is full of people who perceived, correctly or incorrectly, that they had better offers. You have a better offer . . . somewhere. I resent it, it hurts, but I can't blame you.'

'...'

'You don't want to give me your youth. That's okay. I can wait. I'll take the 30s. Even the 40s. I am used to this in life. Waiting. Patience is the thing. And I have patience like a coiled spring set firmly in place. But when it is unset. Oh, when it is. . . .'

'You'll drown me.'

Jonah sighed. 'All you want is an adventure somewhere. On a witch's broom. . . through a sewer pipe. . . I dunno.'

'And you?'

'I want my adventures in the middle of Broadway. In the sun. Taking back. I always wanted to believe I could imagine something to the point of experience.'

'When you were a wittle Jonah?'

'But the intimacy or wonder or revelation I was experiencing - it was always my own. Never shared.'

'Not necessarily bad.'

'I want to walk through the world, witnessing happiness I can share.'

'Or reading.' She smiled. 'Or this.'

He smiled. She smiled.

She showed him how the cow ate cabbage.

City Property

Two young men set beach chairs on the sidewalk, opposite the school's front lawn. The tall one wore a black T-shirt branded with either a rock band's name or a sarcastic slogan, in white block letters: City Property. The shorter one wore an untucked dress shirt and tie, perhaps wanting to lend credibility to the endeavor.

City Property rested heavily a large cooler between the colorful beach chairs, on Midland Avenue; while Tie rummaged about a black backpack, eventually producing a stack of cardboard party hats. Without looking up from the pack, he handed a hat to City Property. The fire station to their backs (across the one way Floral Parkway) was made of the sort of cement that looked like brick; a bumpy gelatinous mass of poured brick.

I recognized the two of them from many years ago. Although I was never certain of it, as Custodian of the school I had probably cleaned up vomit from just about every student who passed through. I'm not sure what this means about the school, if anything. When I come across a student grown into adulthood, he holds the certainty of this happening over me, much like I hold it over him.

I was sitting in Mrs. Yard's room, or what was the room she had taught Social Studies and Economics in for several decades. Her large brown desk was the final item in the room - and the school entire - which had otherwise been cleared for the demolition. I had checked over each room, with a thorough checklist, five times.

I was seated at Mrs. Yard's brown desk, my legs pressed against the desk's guts, where it was hollowed for a seated figure to fill.

I looked through the enormous window-frame of Mrs. Yard's second floor classroom, the cars traversing the highway on the mountain in the distance. The window-frame had been relieved of glass only moments before in the only violent riot I had allowed myself in an otherwise patient and calm process of preparing for the demolition. The window framed much of the front lawn of the campus, which was not large and looked crowded with only a flagpole and two trees as decoration.

The last items to come down from the walls when Mrs. Yard moved out were the large rectangular puzzles she had put together, and then laminated. And which I had hung intermittently, after she had finished them at home and brought them to school. I had climbed the school's wooden ladder to put them up, and to take them down. Along the upper perimeter of the four walls, large empty rectangular shapes - a lighter shade of the wall's dreary and comforting blue paint - sat in the puzzles' places.

Before sunrise that morning I had run the two flags up the flagpole, and watched as they billowed and whispered over the cool lawn. Their shadows creating dark waves on the grass. That they whispered was significant enough; let alone what they whispered. I was tempted to fly them at half-mast, but did not. The day was not entirely mournful, as the boys in the beach chairs on Midland Avenue reminded me. City Property and Tie gleefully toasted each other with beverages wrapped in brown paper bags.

The pocked ebony wrecking ball hung like a marble moon outside the fourth and last window of the classroom. I was looking through papers I had found in Mrs. Yard's desk, but could not distract myself from the wrecking ball. I imagined what it might be like to bite into it, and break my teeth into bits. Or to actually make purchase with my teeth, and let the rough surface itch my swollen gums. This was not an institution that afforded a Custodian dental insurance.

City Property and Tie looked young, not yet even thirty. The oldest possible graduate of the school would have been sixty at most. The small shabby peach-painted house behind the two boys was another in the neighborhood that had lost its attractiveness, its liveliness. And thus its livelihood.

The two sat in beach chairs and drank. City Property lit a cigar, and passed one to Tie, who seemed to prefer cigarettes. They wore wonderful smiles, and made heraldic toasts, with great eagerness and contagious repetition.

I heard the brief but unmistakable cough of the awakening of the crane's engine, as the crew meandered about. They held paper cups of steaming coffee, as well as cigarettes, creating a placid mist around their heads. Stems of sun pushed through the mist and bounced from their sunglasses and hard hats.

Hearing the crane, the two young men stood up and began to cheer; to jump in place excitedly, pumping their fists encouragingly towards the crew. Tie produced party whistles from his pack, and they squealed in unison as the crane began to move towards the school. Some pedestrians passing by on Midland Avenue turned their heads and watched the two, before quickening their pace with perplexed and fearful expressions. I heard a shrill but distinctive 'Whee!' or 'Wha-hoo!' over the sound of the crane.

The foreman walked from the crane to the front steps of the school and pulled on the two doors, which were locked. A ritualistic superstition, he'd explained before. He stepped back and looked up to the empty window-frame, removing his sunglasses and squinting.

'Peter?' he called to me, his eyebrows questioningly raised, his arm extending a questioning thumbs-up gesture.

'I have not changed my mind,' I said. I extended a thumbs-up out of the window-frame.

'Let's rock,' the foreman shouted, walking away.

The wrecking ball began wrecking the northwest corner of the building. The classroom trembled. City Property and Tie exchanged repeated high-fives and relentless toasting, each toast successively more complex than the previous one. Behind the back toast. Between the legs. Stand on your head. City Property discarded his party whistle in favor of beverage access. Four empty cans and a pile of used whistles lay scattered on the sidewalk at their feet.

The U.S. flag whipped and snapped over the lawn. I had rescued that particular flag from the school's furnace when the previous, and final, school year had begun. Shop and Crafts classes were sometimes offered in what was known as the Custodian's Office, which was just an enormous room in the school's labyrinth of a basement, where the immense furnace and my desk both sat.

The papers I had found in Mrs. Yard's desk were assignments from students, all dated May 17, 1985. The children had been asked to write about current events, and what life was like for normal people in the United States. One had written about pending legislation for a shorter work week. Another about the coming minor league baseball season for his favorite hometown team, the Chiefs. One child wrote about the bombing of Philadelphia residents by the Philadelphia Police Department. I thought even the largely illegible penmanship of these assignments looked dated, and out of vogue.

    Closing my eyes and listening, I surmised that the wrecking ball was wrecking the southeast corner of the school. Three-fourths done. The foreman and I had discussed their wrecking plans the day before. He was an understanding man. Most of the crew were hanging about on the east lawn, where soccer games had sometimes been played. Three of the crew were standing at equal intervals along the sidewalk on Midland Avenue, prohibiting access to the two driveways with orange cones. And prohibiting access to the lawn with a long band of yellow crime scene tape, stretching from the No Parking sign near the Arctic Island ice cream place, to the No Parking sign in front of the abandoned house next to the school's parking lot. The crew seemed to decline notice of the two young men.

    The Christian flag snapped, beneath the U.S. flag. I regretted not having thought to donate the Christian flag to the Methodist church down the block, where I knew they needed one.

    A sudden crash of matter that sounded like innumerable coins falling to the floor or a woman screaming suddenly overwhelmed me, and then there was a dramatic stillness. Tie removed a cigar from his shirt pocket and began lighting it. Puff puff. The two flags flapped at each other, their corners smartly whipping and cracking. The three crew members on Midland Avenue turned their backs to the building stoically. Only one remained from the gaggle on the east lawn, perhaps the rest buying ice cream at Arctic Island, whose neon sign I barely glimpsed over the abandoned house at campus' edge. City Property opened a can and consumed it without relent and opened another, laughing riotously between, his lips foamy.

The yellow crane crept from the east wall to the north; settling for a moment below me and the classroom. The crane hummed fiercely, as though making penultimate exhalations of satisfaction. The crane operator counted to sixty, as prearranged, and extended a thumbs-up towards me with a huge gloved hand. I returned the thumb.

It did not sound like glass breaking or bombs exploding or frozen meteorites colliding. It did not sound like floorboards dropping or bricks thudding or steel snapping. Tie jumped up and down on the sidewalk as though it were made of springs, and he were made of ecstasy. My eye burned catching the bright sun's reflection from the wrecking ball. It did not feel like ascension. City Property belched and Tie danced, madly.

Thwack

The squeak of the windshield sounded like children laughing. She was driving because he had had many beers at the reception. Frogs were jumping from the roadside into the road in heedless efforts to cross the curiously busy rural road. He had been watching their long legs extend behind their airborne bodies for several miles now, the frogs' silhouettes against the headlight lit brush and grass of the roadside. She didn't mind driving because it meant she didn't have to talk. He was loquaciously inebriated, though alert enough to not mention the frogs, knowing it would horrify her. How she could not hear the thudding they made - on the car ahead and on their own as the bodies bounced and thwacked on all sides and tops and bottoms - was up to her.

He was in the process of responding to her query, What did you talk to Pastor Dan about for so long?

Well Pastor Dan, he went on, I've known Pastor Dan since-. Well he's always been this peripheral figure in the midst of my mist, this morass of-. So for like fifteen years I've known this guy though I've spent less time with him in those fifteen years than I have with you in these three months. He affectionately removed his hand from his crotch to gently squeeze her thigh. See Pastor Dan wasn't my pastor but Manfred's who I knew through Kayeef. Like Keith, but not Keith. I named him that in the sixth grade and it stuck. But Pastor Dan is always, I think, eager to pick my brain a little since he knows my dad is a preacher and that I'm not much into Jesus anymore and I think he likes to-. He likes to hear what the diners have to say about his restaurant.

So I do find it interesting, he continued, to hear what a Christian who I'm not related to has to say about lots of questions I'd like to ask Christians but can't ask people I'm related to. Because I don't like to ask questions of my mom that prompt her to imagine me burning in eternal flames, teeth broken. And doing your laundry is so expensive.

In hell. She played along, stating the question flatly.

Right. It's good to make jokes about hell. Because it's right here. He made a sweeping motion with his hand to show that he meant life, existence, the world. And but in turn Pastor Dan gets to hear the opinion of a person who knows – or used to know – his B-I-B-L-E but does not deem it an authority. Sometimes the analogy I make is that a warden interviews an escaped prisoner to learn how and why the fellow escaped. The why being obvious, right? He patted her thigh again. And so we just chatted about the war – well, both of them; all of them? – and health care and citizen's responsibility and he went on about Islamo-Fascism which I just couldn't *not* roll my eyes and smirk even though I know it's dick to do. Because if you're an outside observer of the whole thing who has killed more of who?

He kept saying 'because' as though she had asked a question, but she had not.

The driver in front of them was the sort that is constantly breaking – the red lights shining on their faces through the windshield – in the midst of doing 45mph on a rural (however busy) road. She liked hearing him talk even if she was not listening. His voice was far less assuming and hungry than AM radio. I like when he touches his crotch and then my thigh. It's a trusting gesture. His breath had been odoriferous from Guinness until he'd started smoking and the windows went down. The mist outside was not rain.

God that bride was just-. She could not think of the word but did not want to interrupt him to ask. Then maybe he'd never get started again. I know how he is. Sulk if you interrupt him as though it means you don't give a shit about anything he has ever or will ever say. She had joined him and Pastor Dan at the table on the deck overlooking Lake Ontario for the last hour of their conversation. She participated when something of interest was said but mostly just looked over the water and shivered, not entirely unenjoyable, in the breeze. How can he stand to go on and on like that with Pastor Dan about all that Christianity? I like to talk about my past, too, but it usually involves *me*, not just the ideas ideas ideas.

Thwack thwack thwack thwack. I hope he doesn't hear me killing all these frogs. He's so sensitive. Probably say some internal prayer imagining all of the frog souls – which he doesn't believe in – floating into the aether. He believes in that though! Aether! Well, I believe in gravity. I just wish this fuckstick would stop breaking every goddamn twenty-. Seconds. God I hope he's not so fucked up I have to save him or nurse him or whatever these goddamn boys want. Is this just an American thing? Since we've got presidents and Jesus and the marines is the whole thing just save or be saved for us? For them? For me? Ah, Jesus. She swatted down the turn signal and passed the car in front along the dotted yellow lines, flicking the signal back up to assume the correct lane again. That cake was too big. I don't like ostentation. The dancing was fun. The squeak of the windshield sounded like eyes blinking.

Thwack.

Jesus used to watch me.

After three months of physical intimacy they were suddenly intimate in many other respects as well, something he had not yet experienced. They spoke about God as though the entity would not send retribution from the kingdom in the sky for speaking with frankness. He mentioned the picture of Jesus that had dominated the wall at the top of the stairs in the parsonage inhabited from 1983 to the present by his parents. The picture was a mass-produced brown frame with Jesus 'drawn' in black ink. I kept my head bowed, he told her as she exhaled a whiskey breath, laying face to face on the unkempt carpet of his small apartment in the dark, I kept my head bowed so ascending the staircase I never really saw the picture, it didn't register in my thoughts. I cannot say, he continued, if I did this bowing of my head on subconscious purpose or not. The corner of her lip smirked in a way he was meant to know meant she was happy about the closeness of their relationship and how they could both relate past problems or difficulties or horrors to the other without fear of shame or either thinking that the other would be damned for what they revealed. But, he continued, her hand gently on his neck, each time I descended the stairs – there were 3 steps then a small landing and a right turn to the last 18 steps, and one was eye-level with the picture when standing on the landing, back to the 18 – each time I descended the stairs I'd see that picture of Jesus as I hopped the 3 steps down to the landing, and I *can* say that I did this subconsciously because I was far too afraid of sudden death from above – like Uzzah – followed by everlasting burning in damnation to ever consciously allow myself to think – and Jesus can read your thoughts, of course – (he could assume she knew about Jesus' telepathy and say 'of course' as she had been a Jehovah's Witness for some 18 years of her own lifetime) but my subconscious or whatever in me that would say the thing that I *wouldn't* say would, when I saw the picture of Jesus at the top of the stairs (her hand was no longer just making passes at his zipper) say, 'Fuck you, Jesus.' His heart rate intensified not only because her hand was less than austere but because it had not ceased or even paused in its activities even when he'd gotten to the punch line of 'Fuck you, Jesus.' And so, he continued, all those 18 steps down – it was kind of steep, the staircase, and short steps – all 18 steps to the door I'd be feeling Jesus' eyes from the picture and from heaven sending holy laser beams into the back of my head and I'd just be waiting for Jesus to telepathically (or however it is done) to make my heart fail or break an ankle and me reeling down the stairs my head crashing into the door at the bottom neck broken or my kidneys burst or whichever way He wanted to; Jesus can kill you lots of ways.

She said, Did Jesus used to watch you do this? He used to watch me. He's watching us right now. He's watching us as I-

At the Beach

A woman, VICTORIA (21) and a man, JONAH (26) sit on a beach together, in sand, facing the audience. Umbrellas perch over their heads and an icebox sits stage left. Victoria wears a bikini top and shorts, expensive sunglasses and flip-flops. Jonah wears an old, white undershirt and shorts. Jonah is smoking a cigarette while Victoria leans back, trying to get tanned. She has a hand down Jonah's shorts.

There are three other couples sitting around on the stage, conversing intermittently and sunbathing.

Victoria: I'm not saying you suck, I'm saying your writing sucks.

Jonah: What's the difference?

Victoria: You can't be that dramatic.

Jonah: Can't I?

Victoria: Can you?

Jonah: You've read my stories. How many ex-girlfriends have I mangled, strangled, desecrated with knives or bullets, sent shockingly into unGodly automobile accidents or meaningfully unpleasant sexual experiences with men far less debonair, patient, understanding, attractive and giving than I?

Victoria: A couple?

Jonah: And all after having ravaged them with Don

Juan's own blade.

Victoria: I thought you had to be able to experience something before you could write about it.

Jonah: That's hilarious.

Victoria: Do you want to remove those?

Jonah: The braids? God, yes.

Victoria: It was just an experiment.

Jonah: Pubes shouldn't be braided to look like a Rastafarian.

Victoria: We know that now.

Jonah: Please, go ahead, take them out.

Victoria: But no, I didn't mean the braids, I meant your unders. It would make this easier.

Jonah: Well we're at the beach, it shouldn't be easier. It's whole essence is in the idea that it's difficult to do, subversive, an open secret.

Victoria: Just take them off.

Jonah: Frankly, I don't know that I can even get anywhere in this endeavor what with you're disdain for my prose.

Victoria: You could climax to a slight breeze from grandma's open mouth.

Jonah: Egads, Vic, that's heinous.

Victoria: So what if I think your prose sucks? Nobody thinks you're Joyce.

Jonah: Mmm, that's entirely arousing. Please, lambaste my poetry and use of syntax.

Victoria: Your poetry, well, if you cared to use meter ever I'd be overjoyed and if you wanna talk about more is more, you're got more colons in your stories than a proctologist sees in a lifetime.

Jonah: Gastroenterologist, you mean?

Victoria: Fucking whatever. Yeah, I didn't know what they were called so went for a close approximation.

Jonah: Is your limbic system entirely disconnected from your nervous?

Victoria: Meaning how can I say detrimental things about your stories while giving you a handjob.

Jonah: Right.

Victoria: Aren't they one in the same, Jonah?

Jonah: *(Beat)* That's gonna take me a minute.

> *Pause.*

Victoria: I mean: Don't you think if you wanted to write good stories you would? But you don't want to write good stories. You want to write great stories, and you know better than I do that if you want to write great stories you know you're probably never going to write a 'great' story, and so you'll probably write a lot of bad ones. Really bad ones.

Jonah: Uh-huh.

Victoria: And if you know this and you're willing to persist in it, then I think that, in a direct way, you like writing bad stories. Or, you like writing stories that everyone will dislike so that you can feel misunderstood or like, segregated.

Jonah: You'd better slow down.

Victoria: Oh, sorry, I wasn't paying attention.

Jonah reaches into the icebox and opens a beer.

Victoria (CONT.): What do you think about that?

Jonah: The explanation?

Victoria: Mm.

Jonah: Very astute.

Victoria: You're, ah ... wilting.

Jonah: Maybe we should pack it up.

Victoria: You want to go?

Jonah: I'm done with the beach. This beach might as well be 1808 to me.

Victoria: But you're a historian specializing in the

Napoleonic Wars.

Jonah: Okay, so the analogy doesn't work with me, specifically. But, you know, come on.

Victoria: Do you want me to finish?

Jonah: Not until you like one of my stories.

Victoria: You know long term celibacy doesn't work for either
of us.

Jonah: Har har.

Victoria: Again, I'm not saying I don't like you, I just don't like your stories.

Jonah: What's the difference?

Victoria: You could climax to a brief glance from a hideous blind woman.

Jonah: What the hell are you talking about?

Victoria: What are *you* talking about?

Jonah: You hating my-

Victoria: Right, I know. Sorry. Come on, let's go.

Jonah: Yeah?

Victoria: Sure, we can finish on the drive home.

Jonah: Fine. But I'm choosing the tunes.

Victoria: No more *Rhapsody in Blue*. We heard it twelve times on the way.

Jonah: Fine. But you're removing the Rasta-braids.

Victoria: Come on, before my limbic system wants to stay.

Jonah: Egads.

Victoria: You can ravage my nervous system at home.

Jonah: With prods and electroshock!

Victoria: With semi-colons and periods! I think the Wheel is on tonight, too.

Victoria stands.

Victoria (CONT.): Last one to the car writes bad prose!

Victoria runs offstage. Jonah stands and gathers up their belongings and walks offstage.

The male from the couple stage right sits up and speaks to the male from the couple stage left.

Male #1: What was with those creeps?

Male #2: Fuckin pervs.

Male #1: Fuckin-a.

Christmas Needs To Come Early This Year

Karl was vacuuming the carpet like I had asked him to do while I flummoxed and flumped the furniture all over the narrow living room, making way for the fake but, to our eyes, gorgeous and redemptive Christmas tree.

'Karl, Jonah,' Manfred, our third roommate, stood in his coat, shoeless, spooning food from a foam plastic container into his mouth with his fingers; he and his fiance Victoria had been out to dinner, 'I know you're both lonely but-'

'Ahem!' Karl cleared his throat forcefully and held the roaring vacuum up with arms outstretched towards Manfred. A warning.

'It's only November-'

'Christmas needs to come early this year.' I said it more to the window-sill I was clearing of grit and low-wage-bachelor debris (cigarette butts, mugs, bits of paper, ash, two copies of *Mad*) than to Manfred. Karl and I had already dusted the high walls with the broom and strung three strands of lights around the room, making a quadruple layer of them, so long did they stretch.

'I don't know about anyone else,' Manfred was not to be ignored, 'but I'm not even done eating my *Halloween* candy, and now, what? Guys. Guys?'

'Ahem! Ack ack ack.' Karl ran the vacuum across the floor and just shy of Manfred's shoeless feet, coughing on the dust and dog-fur storm scattered by the vaccuum.

'I even saw some trees today on the way home, alongside the FDR, that still had green leaves, guys. *Green leaves!*'

'Christmas needs to come early this year.'

'And just ask the dog.' Manfred was insistent.

'Look at him, look at Pressler Dog. Look at neutered Pressler Dog.' Pressler wagged his tail upon hearing his name, mouth open in what could have been a grin but just as easily could have been obliviousness. 'He hasn't even *started* growing in a new coat of fur for the wint-'

'Ack ack ack!' Karl, vacuuming the corner, coughed after a gust from the open window blew some of Pressler's hair – a harvest we walked through and upon daily – into his face.

'The window, guys, the window! The window is *open*!' Manfred ran across the room and pointed to the window in mock but genuine earnest, miming a mime. 'You don't have a window open in Brooklyn at Christmas time!'

'Christmas needs to come early this year.' I bit my tongue and waited, hoping to relieve the rising tension within me with flatulence, which did not arrive. In my heart, as little Lord Jesus knew, I was making hilarious if very unkind remarks about *not* having just been to a *bourgeoisie* dinner having romantic and personalizing conversation with a woman who not only gave proletarian handjobs (good ones) but related in some way to the goodtiming but utlimately emotionless male (Manfred) standing before us shoveling some sort of meat and rice into his open maw with three fingers. The tree, I figured, would stand on the empty and rather useless souvenir box.

'Come on, guys, I know it's been-'
'Ahem! Agh! Ack ack ack!'
'-a longer period of isolation, rejection, confusion and meals-for-one than any of us could have imagined, even in our most feverish, thunderous and howling nightm-'

'Ah God, ah God, ack ack ack!' Karl was

vacuuming his pant legs, which of course needed it, but also gave him something to embrace. It was, if not necessary, at least beneficial, in that he did not need any further succor from us, so we let him be.

'Victoria and I walked through the park tonight-'

'Christmas needs to come early this year.' I rapped on the window to make a noise.

'-and the lawn, the grass was just thick with greenness-'

'Yack hack hack!'

'Come *on*, guys!'

Pressler Dog, standing, put his head low to the ground as though he wanted to whimper in pity and licked Karl's face, easily done as Karl lay huddled on the floor, face already awash in tufts of Pressler hair, stuck to streaks of tears and now to Pressler's saliva. Karl had turned off the vacuum and was spooning the appliance, which was at least two feet shorter than he.

'Guys,' Manfred warily eyed the decorations we had taped or stapled or hung from the walls, including the Christmas Ghost, which our married and departed former compatriot and roommate Derik had made two years ago from tissue and dental floss (to cinch the head and give it form), 'Guys, we've barely finished celebrating Columbus Day and not even *close* to the celebration of the Pequot Indian massacre and you wanna-'

'Away in a manger – ack, ack – no crib for a place to sleep-'

'Karl, really.'

'It's a bed, Karl,' I said, 'no crib for a *bed*.'

Pressler had unceremoniously crumpled himself onto the floor, his tail in Karl's face.

'Go tell it on the – ack, ack, agh! – mountain-

'I harmonized.
'-Over the hills and everywhere.'
'Agh!'
'Jesus Christ you guys.'
'Jesus Christ is born,' we finished in harmony. 'That's right, Manfred. That's right, Karl. Go tell it on the mountain. I'll shout it from the windows!'

'Jonah, you don't even like Jesus.'
'Christmas needs to come early this year.'
'-holy night – agh! yack, hog! – all is calm – ... – utz! – all is...'
'Bright, Karl. All is bright.'
'He's gonna lose it on the virgin part.'
Manfred chewed the last of his leftovers loudly, swishing the food down with beer.
'I'm gonna lose it on the virgin part.'
'Me, too,' Manfred said.

I stooped and retrieved Karl, slinging his left arm over my back like a wounded Hollywood soldier carried from a battlefield. Manfred clasped Pressler Dog's front legs and walked with him – sort of inverted wheelbarrow style – and we harmonized in the November night, windows open to the chilly breeze and street illumination, somewhere up above our heads the dull Christmas star, which died light years ago, twinkling.

House On Fire

'The house is on fire. The house is on fire. The house is on fire.'

I said it three times.

I said it three times because I was only four years old and what would I know about a house or a fire, let alone the two together?, and so I better say it more than once and more than twice, even, and Peter said it three times.

GK said, 'No it's not,' adjusting himself more comfortably on the brown couch in the living room and focusing his eyes on the magazine that separated his face from the glowing television screen.

Dad said, 'I'm working on it,' and closed his eyes again to pray that it might rain a tremendous flood that would dowse the flames eating our roof. I asked why he didn't pray for the fire department to come by, which might make for a quicker end to the fire and less inconvenience for the rest of the town who might not want houses submerged in a flood from the Lord to satisfy the flames on the parsonage roof, but he shushed me away with a squinty-eyed scolding.

Many years before I was born Dad had been in Venezuela with Aunt Miriam & Uncle Aaron, in the mission field. Grampa called it, 'Venz-a-way-la,' and paid for the trip. Gram and Grampa's house, which was on fire, sat just ten feet from the thin road. In rural Maine, ten feet was a breath, most houses giving the road a quarter-mile breadth or more. The house was built on a small hill that looked as though it was molded (the hill) to fit the foundation of the house. Beyond the front porch the lawn around the house swept down from the road and house, so that in winter we would sled from the road and on down the brief but steep hill that leveled into a backyard and finally a forest, itself rushing down to a small river we were never to go down to, ever. From the lawn, between Grampa's garage and the house, I watched first smoke and then fire appear on the rooftop. I hoped momentarily that we had a fire place, but we did not.

'It's just the fireplace,' Mom said. 'Let's ask the Lord to send down the rain to stop the fire in the fireplace.' I wanted to ask why we didn't put it out ourselves, but that would have meant acquiescing to the existence of a fireplace, which we did not have.

GK told me to shut up about it and to call the fire department myself if it would yank my chain. I told him we could probably put the fire out ourselves with some buckets or just the hose that Grandma used to water the flower pots, it was sitting right there outside, we had just drunk from it earlier after playing one-on-one football between the garage and the house. He told me to shut up about it, the house isn't on fire, get out of the way, my show is on.

I shoved open the screen door and walked along the side of the house on the brown porch. I had seen my first titty, consciously, last week on the porch, Aunt Phebe's breast feeding my cousin, Paul, just outside the screen door to the kitchen.

I couldn't smell the smoke yet and so thought the situation wasn't out of hand. I didn't know how quickly a house could burn down. The only fire I had seen was in GK's book, *Disasters of the World*. The cover had a beautiful image of people running away from a massive tower of fire. Probably from a bomb exploding, GK said when I asked. What else explodes?, I thought. When GK was reading the book I'd sit across from him in the living room and stare at the cover, my eyes wobbly, like they were one end of a magnet and the image was the opposite end of a different magnet, and we were not only repelled by each other but also held in immobile collusion together, transfixed.

'Grandpa!' I yelled out over the back railing that Dad had helped Grandpa nail together when we moved in a few months ago. GK was off for summer break but started sixth grade in September. I was pretty sure Grandpa wasn't home but yelled out into the backyard anyway.

The back of the house ran another fifteen feet beyond the porch's end. I felt a strange loss of balance when I looked at the street, which was ground level with me on the porch, and then at the ground in the backyard around the cement base of the house, which was 'Sixteen feet, five inches' below me, according to Grandpa and his yellow measuring tape. When I stood near the street and looked at the house it was two storeys tall. But from the backyard it had a deep and wide basement. I imagined when I called out to Grandpa or whoever else from the back of the porch that my voice moved out and then curved around the house and looked for Grandpa or whoever on the other side of the backyard, too, in case they were there. The lawn ran uphill on that side of the property and on occasion, huffing it up there, I found small trees and bushes and I wasn't allowed to go beyond them. Sometimes when Dad cupped his hands under a stream of water from the faucet or the tap outside I thought of the backyard. A soft bowl.

'Grandpa! Grandpa! The house is on fire!'

'Shut up!' GK called from the couch. I didn't think he'd be able to hear me over the television, especially since you had to open the side door and walk through the kitchen and then the entry room to get to the living room from that corner of the porch.

GK always came into the kitchen and then into the dining room to get to the living room (bypassing the entry room) even though Mom had told us not to wear our dirty sneakers on the nice wood floor of the dining room.

    I sat and wrapped my arms and legs through the balusters of the porch railing and looked across the lawn, parallel to the roadway. I didn't close my eyes or fold my hands together or put my head down. I asked God to make the fire stop somehow. I wasn't concerned with how and wouldn't even ask how it happened if he didn't want me to know, only please make the fire not there anymore, on the roof. Through the thin screen door to the kitchen I heard Mom on the telephone talking to Aunt Miriam. Mom must have been reading GK's book because she was worrying about what if an earthquake made the house crumble?, or a hurricane took it away and placed it somewhere else?, or a meteor or comet hit the house?, and a bunch of other things I worried about sometimes, too.

    'Mom,' I said, peering into the kitchen, 'the house,' pointing to the ceiling and meaning to signify the roof. Mom didn't give me a stern look or put her finger to her lips or say 'Shh', she just turned her back as though I were the refrigerator humming a little louder or the screen door knocking against the frame in the wind. I wondered why she didn't take the one or two seconds to communicate something to me instead of ignoring me, as it was only one or two seconds of her time I needed, respecting that she was on the phone. 'Maybe you can call the fire department next?' I said, waiting a few moments before writing it down on a piece of paper, along with their telephone number, 9-1-1, and walking around Mom's back so that we were face to face and I could hand her the piece of paper and she could read it and nod to me or in some quiet, unobtrusive-to-the-phone-conversation manner convey to me that she understood what I was communicating.

She turned her back to me immediately as I pointed to the roof and held out the paper, and we spun in a circle for a minute. Eventually she spun the phone cord – it was not wireless – around her body like a cocoon and I walked away.

I made a large sign on poster board in the basement with markers and pens from Grandpa's desk that read, 'Help! Help! The House Is On Fire!' with an arrow pointing towards the house. When I went outside to stand by the road I realized the arrow pointed to the house only for vehicles heading out of town. When I turned, to attract traffic heading into town, the arrow pointed across the street into the bramble of the uninhabited fenceless field that ran up and out of sight. There was more traffic creeping into town than out so I stood facing the former, Grampa's church steeple some ways off behind me blending with the sky and treetops, and hoped the drivers would understand the sign.

One nice man stopped his pickup truck and, scratching his balls and dragging on a cigarette, said, 'Yep, that house is on fiyah. Kid, tell ya mothah.'

'I did, sir.'

'And what'd she do?' He spat onto the road black tobacco spit. He was not afraid to stand in the middle of the road, on the faded yellow lines, even with the corner up ahead and the slope down towards town behind him.

'She prayed and called my Aunt Miriam.'

'Good 'nough,' he said and got back into his truck. 'Tell your fathah, too, kid.'

I set the sign to rest against the mailbox's

post and told Mom and Dad and GK again that the house was on fire. Mom started sweating and called Aunt Orpah and Dad got out the catechism and GK punched me in the stomach and made me get him a can of soda.

'Would soda put out the fire on the roof?' I asked, passing him the sweaty aluminum can.

He told me it would but it would be stupid because you'd waste too much money buying all the soda and water was free, and besides shut up about it the house isn't on fire. I asked if the soda to put the fire out would cost more than the house. He told me to shut up and I went upstairs where Grandma was sleeping in her bedroom. Grandma and Grandpa's bedroom was small like the house was, small like I thought a mouse's bedroom would be small relative to the smallness of the mouse's house. GK had taught me about relativity. Dad called it heresy.

'Grandma?' I said, more to wake her up than to see if she was awake. She had been knitting a quilt in the rocking chair in the corner when she'd fallen asleep and her head hung down over the quilt on her lap, the needle sticking up through the porous blanket. Grandma always fell asleep in rocking chairs, or anywhere else she was. Sometimes in the middle of reading me a story or talking to Dad. 'Grandma? The house is on fire,' I whispered, my hand on her gray slacks which matched her gray sneakers with thick gray soles. Her hands were wrinkled and I slowly traced my fingertips along the veins that protruded as old people's veins do. Her gray and white hair sprouted outwards about her head and I scratched her scalp gently, saying, 'Grandma? The house is on fire.'

'Jonah,' she said, waking, sitting up straight in the rocking chair, a warm soft hand on my shoulder and neck. 'Jonah, what are you up to, sweetie?'

'Grandma, the house is on fire.'

'I know, Jonah. I heard you telling your Mom and Dad that the house was on fire. What did your dad say?'

'He's asking God to send a flood.'

'And your mom?'

'She called Aunt Orpah and Aunt Miriam and I think she called my other Grandma, too. Her mom.'

'And did you tell GK?'

'Yes, but he's watching a show.'

She sighed and lifted me onto her lap.

'Let me call your grandfather,' she said, dialing the rotary phone by the bed.

'Sorry, Lydia,' she said, hanging up after two numbers had been dialed. We had forgotten that Mom was on the phone.

Grandpa was only a half-mile away at the church writing his sermon. I was too young to walk there alone and Grandma was too old, or at least that's what Dad said when she sent me downstairs to tell them she and I could go get Grandpa to put out the fire. Mom, still on the phone, somehow without acknowledging my presence, sent me back upstairs with a cup of coffee for Grandma. Dad said he was wishing the prophets of Baal would come and make fun of him (Dad) and his God so that he could dance around the house and light even more fire to it and then call down the flood from God to show the Baal prophets that his (Dad's) God was mightier, was the *true* God. I asked who the fire-fighters worshipped and he told me not to spill the coffee on the way up the stairs.

When GK was small and would climb onto Grandma's lap while she drank coffee she would

warn him, 'Careful, GK, *hot* coffee, *hot* coffee.'
Eventually GK warned himself for Grandma, saying as he climbed, '*Hot kaka, hot kaka.*'

'He was too little,' Grandma said when I was back on her lap, 'to know what coffee or kaka was, Jonah.' I liked to look at her teeth when she laughed, which were probably of average size though seemed big to me because mine were so small. Her teeth were white, polluted white, with flecks of darkness strewn like crystals in a sidewalk. I thought that Grandma could devour me but I did not think she would do so. And if she did I knew it would be the right thing to do because she would be doing it. It was difficult to find Grandma when she wasn't smiling, even though most of the time she was doing lots of work, like cleaning or cooking or making things.

'Grandma,' I said, 'the house is on fire. What if it burns up?' My chin quivered and it was all right to cry if I had to with Grandma, but I didn't.

'The house won't burn up, Jonah. I think your grandpa will be back in time. But if it does we'll move somewhere else and live somewhere else. The church will build us a new house.'

'But this house has all of our things in it. And our bodies.'

She drank some coffee, carefully eyeing me over the rim to see I didn't make coffee-spilling movements.

'We'll take our bodies out of here and leave our things behind. We don't need them.'

'But my books and my t-shirts, Grandma. And all your pictures. And the picture frames on the wall. And the wallpaper with the stains on it where we all know where the stains are. And the tile in the kitchen Dad said you can't buy any more of 'cause it's old. And your dishes you've had forever. And the couch and Grandpa's brown chair, Grandma-'

I lay my head on her chest and she drank from the white mug. I could hear her body, her heartbeat and other noises I didn't know what they were, through her gray sweatshirt. I closed my eyes and it felt like nighttime when the windows were open and the rain descended like a vast, penetrable sheet.

'Grandma, if we die will we know each other in heaven?'

'I don't know, Jonah. But we'll be all right. Whatever heaven is like.'

'Do you think it will be like the world?'

'Oh, it will be much better, Jonah. Much better.'

When Grandpa got home I ran downstairs and told him the house was on fire. He picked me up and held me by my armpits above his head, laughing. I took his pocket comb from his shirt pocket and combed the thin rim of hair around his otherwise bald head and then combed it with my fingers and ran the back of my hands along his face, which was never bearded but always softly scratchy. Grandpa laughed in triplet exhalations. 'Hey hey hey. Hey hey hey.' He rarely laughed at jokes or stories, but just from seeing someone or doing something fun.

'Grandpa, the house is on fire and Mom's on the phone and Dad is running around the house waiting for prophets of Baal and then the flood and GK is watching his show and Grandma said you could-'

He set me down and we walked out the front door, where he'd just come in, and a little ways from the house surveyed it. Dad ran by howling and laughing and saying something like, 'Came in a

Hyundai, left in a Hyundai,' really fast, which we sometimes heard at churches that weren't ours. I didn't see any Baal prophets and hoped Dad wouldn't be disappointed if we put out the fire without God.

Walking around to the side of the house where I hardly ever ventured the lawn swept up to the bushes and trees. Grandpa said, 'Good eye, Jonah,' and picked me up and held me to his hip while he walked. 'Its eaten up almost the whole back of the roof. Can you smell that, Jonah?' whiffing the air. I nodded and breathed deeply several times to show that I was smelling it.

'Grandpa,' as we both unwound the hose from its circular mooring, 'how come God won't come down and put the fire out?'

He didn't say anything but sprayed me a little with the hose, to make me laugh before pointing it upwards at the roof. We heard the sizzle of hot tiles being made wet.

A caravan of six cars pulled up and settled in single file in the parking area between the house and the garage, where Grandpa had cleared the grass and lain special stones and dirts to keep the hill from crumbling away so visitors could park there. Dad ran out to them hoping they were the prophets of Baal. Grandpa walked to the front of the house, leaving me to hold the hose, and smiled and waved to people exiting the cars and called out some of their names. They were the group of pastors, all around Grandpa's age, who ministered in churches around our town, Peru. Most of the preachers were from Oxford County, but some came from as far away as Penobscot and Aroostook because they were old friends with Grandpa and liked the monthly meetings held at our house. They would merrily sit around the dining room table and drink coffee, tea, milk, juice, water and eat crackers, chips, small sandwiches, cookies, ice cream.

I heard the washing machine in the basement end its cycle, which produced greater water pressure for the hose than I could control. As I struggled to maintain the flow to the flames on the roof water flew into the kitchen through the far window where Mom was on the phone. She yelled out the window to quit fooling around with the hose and that I had put out the burners on the stove's top which was heating water for coffee and tea. Grandma's window was on the other side of the house so she didn't get wet. I heard her calling out the window to my dad to get the ladder from the garage and carry the hose up to the roof. He told her she was only seeking the human solution. GK came outside when all the cars showed up and took the hose from me and I had to run up to the bushes and trees to get out of his range.

'GK, point it at the roof. Look!'

He looked up and shrugged, saying, 'It's fine.'

'GK, the house is on fire!'

'No, it's not.'

He tossed the flowing hose onto the lawn and walked back inside.

'Dad!' I called when he rounded the corner of the house, running. I was trying to warn him about the blazing wood shingle that was falling from the roof and that landed flat on his head while he ran. Blinded, he collided with the birdfeeder outside the dining room window and fell on his back, his body rigid.

GK had run outside and got to Dad before I did, grabbing an unlit corner of the shingle and whipping wildly it away from him and Dad and through the dining room window, which crashed and

made very loud sounds. The tile continued through
the doorless doorway to the kitchen and passed
Mom, just below the taut phone cord, then through
the screen on the screen door, over the porch railing
and into the lawn. Mom shrieked, yelling, 'That tile is
on fire!' and dropping the phone ran outside with the
full teapot to put out the tile.

    Dad wasn't unconscious, only stunned and
was quickly on his feet again.

    'Dad?' I said. 'The house?'

    Dad shook his head to clear it and walked to
the flowing hose, soaking his feet in the expanding
puddle, and aimed the water at the roof, which
sizzled. I jumped and cheered. But before the fire
was out six prophets of Baal emerged in red robes
from the forest behind the house and started
chanting and asking Baal to put out the fire. Dad
dropped the hose and started praying on his own,
head bowed eyes closed hands folded together,
asking God to make the fire worse, to send down
more fire, and then to put it out. I tried to get GK to
hold the hose to put out the last of the fire but he was
aiming it at Dad's head to cool it off from the hot tile.

    I walked inside and upstairs into Grandma's
room and woke her up by saying her name and took
her by the hand and we walked down the stairs
through the front door beyond the porch up the
stone walkway across the road and into the field up
the hill. We sat in a dry patch of dirt and yellow
grasses and watched GK chase Dad with the hose
and the prophets of Baal chanting in a circle and
Mom on the phone the cord stretched to the porch
through the screen door and Grandpa and his friends
mingling on the front lawn talking and examining
delicate, ancient texts.

    'You should have gotten your books, Jonah.

We didn't think ahead.'

So she recited some stories she knew from when she taught English class before she retired, and we watched the house and everyone around it, and the Lord came down when the rain descended to send quiffs and quaffs and plumes of smoke jettisoning and whispering from the house's wet breath of ashes.

I asked Grandma, as the smoke looked beautiful around us, if, in the new world, there would be books, or would we all know everything already? And wouldn't it get boring up there with nothing to do but praising God all the time, because that sounded like any old regular Sunday morning and she knew how I felt about those. It was okay to tell Grandma that you didn't like Sunday mornings.

Grandma said, 'I don't know, Jonah. But in the new world there will be sounds. Trumpets. Shouts of joy and love for God.'

I laughed and said I didn't think she ever wanted to shout ever. Shout like me, Grandma?'

'No, not like you, Jonah. Not even when you are running around the backyard with sticks and stories in your head. Shouts that are the release of the cold dignity of silence. Shouts that have been screamed for many many years, and many many times, without ever having made a sound. But those will become shouts of glory for the Lord, Jonah. We will be the shouting. We will be the trumpets.'

I asked Grandma if we would be like Shadrach, Meschach, and Abednego, and the smell of the fire wouldn't stick to us. She laughed and asked since when was I worried so much about smell? I laughed and said I hoped Dad didn't do like Elijah after Mount Carmel with the prophets of Baal in the brook in the forest.

notes

'It Was Me' and 'Thwack' appear in altered form in the author's novel *Boulevardiers: The Greenpoint Oil Spill*.

Words from 'Iko Iko' by The Dixie Cups (1963).

Words from 'Helena' by Sordid Humor (1994).

other works by the author

Boulevardiers: The Greenpoint Oil Spill - The first novel atop the Greenpoint Oil Spill.

Made in the USA
Columbia, SC
17 September 2023